KT-582-435

WITHDRAWN
FROM
DONCASTER
LIBRARY SERVICE

DONCASTER LIBRARY SERVICE

30122 01352570 0

-6 FEB 1995

WITHDRAWN
FROM
DONCASTER
LIBRARY SERVICE

SPECIAL MESSAGE TO READERS

This book is published by
THE ULVERSCROFT FOUNDATION,
a registered charity in the U.K., No. 264873

The Foundation was established in 1974 to provide funds to help towards research, diagnosis and treatment of eye diseases. Below are a few examples of contributions made by THE ULVERSCROFT FOUNDATION:

★ A new Children's Assessment Unit at Moorfield's Hospital, London.

★ Twin operating theatres at the Western Ophthalmic Hospital, London.

★ The Frederick Thorpe Ulverscroft Chair of Ophthalmology at the University of Leicester.

★ Eye Laser equipment to various eye hospitals.

If you would like to help further the work of the Foundation by making a donation or leaving a legacy, every contribution, no matter how small, is received with gratitude. Please write for details to:

THE ULVERSCROFT FOUNDATION,
The Green, Bradgate Road, Anstey,
Leicestershire, LE7 7FU. England.
Telephone: (0533) 364325

Love is
a time of enchantment:
in it all days are fair and all fields
green. Youth is blest by it,
old age made benign: the eyes of love see
roses blooming in December,
and sunshine through rain. Verily
is the time of true-love
a time of enchantment—and
Oh! how eager is woman
to be bewitched!

THE DARK SUMMER

When Janice Prior returns to spend a convalescent holiday with her aunt, the last person she expects to meet in the Dorset village is Mark Galbraith, her first love, who has since married. After all, their poignant teenage romance was over and done with long ago. Or was it? The first meeting with Mark leaves Jan in no doubt.

NANCY BUCKINGHAM

THE DARK SUMMER

Complete and Unabridged

ULVERSCROFT
Leicester

First published in Great Britain in 1968

First Large Print Edition
published May 1990

Copyright © 1968 by Nancy Buckingham
All rights reserved

British Library CIP Data

Buckingham, Nancy
    The dark summer.—Large print ed.—
Ulverscroft large print series: romance, suspense
I. Title
823'.914[F]

ISBN 0-7089-2199-X

DONCASTER LIBRARY AND
INFORMATION SERVICE

013525700

ᴜᴋᴠ	19 JAN 1995
ʟᴘ	£ 8·25

Published by
F. A. Thorpe (Publishing) Ltd.
Anstey, Leicestershire
Set by Rowland Phototypesetting Ltd.
Bury St. Edmunds, Suffolk
Printed and bound in Great Britain by
T. J. Press (Padstow) Ltd., Padstow, Cornwall

1

"I FORGET, Jan," said my Aunt Frank, emerging suddenly from her preoccupation with the *Oxford Dictionary*. "Did you ever meet Mark Galbraith?"

She just didn't realize how funny that question was. *Did I ever meet Mark?* Only every single day of that time five years ago I'd stayed here at her cottage in Dorset. And thought about him and dreamed about him every night too! It had been a bitter-sweet young love, and when Mark and I tore ourselves apart on that last evening, I was certain that my heart was broken and would never mend.

It all seemed so infinitely long ago and I could look back without pain. Only tender wonder at such intensity of loving.

I could even talk about it now, so I grinned at Aunt Frank.

"Yes, I met Mark all right. As a matter of fact, he was my first boy friend. We had quite a little romance that summer."

"Did you now?" She looked surprised. "Then perhaps it's just as well I knew nothing at the time, or I'd have felt I should do something about it. Being in charge of you, I mean. After all, you were only . . . seventeen, then."

But she wouldn't have known what to do. To Aunt Frank "romance" was just a seven letter word beginning with "r". A useful enough word in the crosswords she compiled for a Sunday newspaper. I could imagine the sort of clue she'd give—*"There's a man in this disjointed core."*

Already she was absorbed again in her reading, but I couldn't leave it at that.

"Why did you ask?" I said, still smiling up at her from my rug on the lawn.

"Ask what?"

"If I'd met Mark Galbraith."

"Oh, didn't I tell you? He'll be at the Buxtons' with his mother this evening."

I thought I'd got over Mark long ago, but the sudden racing of my pulses astonished and disturbed me. The prospect of meeting him this very evening was—I didn't know what. Exciting . . . or alarming?

There were questions I longed to ask,

but by now Aunt Frank's elusive attention was firmly switched to its own business again. I saw that she hadn't changed. My aunt would come and go like this throughout the day, and normally it didn't bother me a bit. It was so easy to be a guest in her house, for she didn't allow my being there to interfere with her ordinary life. I knew my company was welcome enough to her, but she didn't *need* me. She didn't need anybody. Aunt Frank was the most self-contained woman I'd ever known.

As patiently as I could, I waited for an opportunity to ask what Mark was doing in Bishop's Cranford.

I'd hardly thought about Mark Galbraith these last couple of years. The news of his marriage had neatly tied off any loose ends of our romance that may have been lying around in my mind. Besides, I'd had plenty of other things to think about.

After completing my year's secretarial course at College, I'd gone out to the Middle East. My father was a technical adviser with Anglo-Kutainian Oil, and a job as secretary to one of his colleagues was lined up for me.

Altogether life in Kutain was larger than any girl had the right to expect. I lived in the luxurious comfort of my parents' home, and my salary was ample to provide me with all the clothes I fancied, and even a car of my own. My leisure was filled with parties and swimming and tennis, and there was an endless belt of bronzed, handsome men—American, British, and an occasional Italian to add Latin spice.

My mother, herself happily married at twenty, simply couldn't understand how I had reached the ripe old age of twenty-two without a fiancé even on the horizon. To her mind I wasn't trying. Night after night when I got home she would look at me questioningly, hoping I had a proposal to report. She knew her over-anxiety irritated me, but poor Mother couldn't restrain herself. "It's just that I'm interested, darling," she would protest. "After all, it's only natural. I want you to be happy."

Like so many of the leisured European women in Kutain, Mother spent her time following the progress of each budding

4

romance in the colony, speculating about the prospects. She'd always been like that.

It's something of a family joke that she once tried to find a husband for Aunt Frank. Flushed with the success of her own marriage, she longed to bring equal happiness to her spinster sister-in-law. Where better, she confided to Dad, than Kutain, where eligible men were plentiful, and unmarried women in short supply. A pressing invitation was despatched to England forthwith.

The cunning strategem seemed certain of success. In spite of Aunt Frank's eccentric personality; in spite of her thickset figure and purposeful gait, there were soon several suitors lined up and eager. And they got nowhere, nowhere at all. Apparently, she didn't turn them down; she just didn't seem to notice their advances.

Myself, I was never left in any doubt about the men's advances. I didn't dare report to Mother the several proposals I turned down, or she'd really have gone off the deep end. It wasn't that I didn't like any of the men—in fact, I liked some of them a lot. But somehow I always stopped short of getting myself further involved than a fairly mild flirtation. Maybe I wasn't ready for marriage. I don't know!

Still, everything was going very nicely for me until I was suddenly laid low by a violent bout of enteritis. In that heat an illness can really pull you down, and I felt quite washed out. The doctor advised a spell back home.

"You need a few weeks in a nice temperate climate," he said. As he wiped his sweating forehead he added with a grin, "England in April! I wish someone would prescribe that for me."

I knew just what he meant. The dryness and brassy sun of Kutain does depress you after a time. The prospect of a spell in the lush countryside of England seemed highly attractive.

Only one thing bothered me. I had recently been promoted, and was now personal secretary to Bill McKinlay, one of the top men out there. It was a plum job, and I didn't want to risk losing it.

"Don't you worry about that, Janice," Bill had said when he visited me at home. "I'll fill in with a temp while you're away. There's nobody else can save me the job of composing letters the way you do."

With that friendly assurance, I was in a pretty happy mood as I prepared for what seemed more like a holiday than convalescence. It had been fixed for me to stay with Aunt Frank in Dorset.

I was to travel home on the *Kutain Rose*, one of the big new tankers. The Company always looked after its employees at every turn, and provided super accommodation on its vessels. What with staff going on leave or taking up appointments elsewhere, there was always a number of passengers.

As my parents and I stood on deck awaiting the "visitors ashore" call, Mother, game to the end, had been surveying the male potential.

"Oh darling, look over there," she whispered, suddenly excited. "It's that nice young man from records, Peter Stretton. The voyage will give you a chance of getting to know him better."

"If he's got any sense," I remarked sourly, "he'll concentrate on girls who aren't liable to keel over at the slightest provocation." The mere effort of getting myself on board had proved just how weak

7

I still was. "I'm a pretty lousy catch for any man at the moment."

Mother's frown reprimanded me. "Nonsense, Jan darling. A few days' sea air will do you the world of good. And then a couple of months with your Aunt Frank in Bishop's Cranford! You'll come back absolutely bursting with health, you'll see." But being Mother she couldn't resist adding an arch rider. "That is, unless you meet someone over there and . . ."

"Mother! You're incorrigible!" As I gave her a fond farewell hug I caught my father's wink.

It had looked like being the tranquil holiday I expected. Aunt Frank met the boat at Southampton, and drove me back to Bishop's Cranford. My first sight of the village as we rounded the bend was like a homecoming. After the monotonous uniformity of a bustling new oil town, such diversity in the old buildings was refreshing. Mead Cottage itself was reputed to be over three hundred years old, and looked like a tea cosy, its white-washed walls and exposed black beams topped with thatch.

8

I settled down to the rest the doctor had prescribed. The sun, which Aunt Frank pronounced to be hot, was deliciously cool on my skin. I felt at peace with the world.

Until three o'clock in the afternoon of the first day!

We were sitting outside in the garden— a quite small patch surrounding the cottage, the little lawn sloping away on its south side. Aunt Frank had brought out a folding canvas chair, and I'd spread a rug on the grass. I lay there lazily, propped on my elbows, picking out the familiar village landmarks against a backcloth of the rolling hills beyond. Our conversation had been intermittent. In one of her short bursts of communication, Aunt Frank told me we had been invited to the Buxtons' for drinks later on.

"How nice," I said. "I've been looking forward to seeing them again."

"It won't be too much for you dear, will it?" my aunt asked anxiously.

I told her not to worry, I was really feeling very fit.

She nodded. "Just the family, you know, and Lionel's sister, Margaret Galbraith."

Even this mention of Mark's mother I received equably, for in a small village community, it was inevitable that I should meet her soon.

It was when Aunt Frank went on to mention that Mark would be there too that I had suddenly been jerked out of my calm. Emotion that I had long thought dead stirred deep inside me.

I'd have expected Mark to be well away from this sleepy corner of England, carving a brilliant career for himself in London. When we had parted, five years ago, he'd been about to start reading Economics at University. I didn't need to ask how well Mark had done—I just knew he would have sailed through the course to an honours degree.

So what was he doing in Bishop's Cranford?

Aunt Frank had disappeared into the cottage, leaving me lying on my rug on the grass, only pretending to read. I could hear her chatting with Mrs. Bird, who came in on three afternoons a week to do the cleaning. I noticed Mrs. Bird was doing most of the talking.

That first time I had stayed with Aunt

Frank, just finished school, I was diffident and a little anxious because to me then my aunt was a formidable figure, largely of legend. I didn't know that beneath her alarming cleverness, behind the brusque detachment she presented to the world, lay a wealth of kindness. It had been an emergency arrangement. I was going to spend the holidays in Kutain as usual before coming back to England to start Business College. Then at the last moment a cable from Mother told me that Dad had been taken ill, not seriously, but enough to send him to hospital. She had gone to stay nearby. Thinking it wouldn't be much fun out there, she arranged for me to stay with Aunt Frank.

Bishop's Cranford had seemed deadly dull at first. But soon I was relishing the unusual taste of freedom. At boarding school every minute of every day was carefully planned, and the holidays in Kutain were a social whirl. Mother was anxious to crowd in every possible entertainment.

Aunt Frank treated me as fully adult. She left me to amuse myself, but not before doing two things that had a significant effect on my stay with her. With some sort of odd inspiration she presented me with a bicycle; and she introduced me to some friends of hers, the Buxton family, which gave me the *entrée* to the life of the village.

Sally Buxton was just my own age, her brother Derek three years older. Their real parents had been killed in a road accident when they were quite young, and they had been brought up by their uncle and aunt with all the love a disappointed childless couple could shower upon them.

Sally was a dumpy girl without particular prettiness. But she radiated friendliness like a fire radiates warmth—unselectively, touching everyone within range. She was always surrounded by a crowd anxious to bask in her glow. At seventeen she was utterly unsophisticated, largely unconscious of the growing tension between the sexes. It wasn't surprising that Sally became the focal point of the young set of Bishop's Cranford, with her aunt's open-house as their base.

We went for picnics, we went swimming, we played badminton on the slightly bumpy grass in the garden. We played pop records in the den, or mooched about in the orchard. The composition of the gang varied from day to day, but I soon noticed that Sally's cousin, Mark Galbraith, always seemed to be there. I soon began noticing everything about Mark. And, miracle of miracles, Mark noticed me!

Inevitably, I suppose, there is a special sweetness, a glimpse of heaven about a first love; that time the heart is awakened. All at once the world became a wonderful, more beautiful place. Overnight I grew up. I knew a unity with all women. I discovered the exquisite pain, the tremulous joy of loving a man.

A breathless quality lingers in my memory about those long hot summer days. Perhaps our love was all the sweeter and more poignant because my heart understood it was only a fleeting golden dream. I knew all the time that it could not last. I knew Mark was not ready for love. For four whole years he would be at University, engrossed in study. It would be four whole years before he could even make a start with his career and think about taking on the responsibility of a wife. To the impatient, possessive love of seventeen it seemed like a lifetime. Our love was too urgent, too fierce, to survive such waiting.

These echoes of the past made me restless. On a sudden whim I got up from my rug and wandered down the garden path to the shed hidden behind the rhododendrons. Felix, the big black and white cat, was sunning himself on the tin roof. I remembered him as a gay bachelor, and now he was a dozy old gentleman cat. I reached up in friendly fashion to tickle him, and he dropped a lazy paw, still ready to be playful.

My bicycle was where Mark had put it that last day! I had to shift a collection of garden tools to get at it. A stack of flower pots was piled crazily upon the saddle, and from the handlebars hung a battered wooden trug.

I wheeled the stiffly protesting machine out into the sunshine, strongly conscious that Mark's had been the last hands to touch it. The bicycle was not an elegant sight. The chromium plating was green, and rust flaked the black enamel in places. The tyres were quite flat, of course. I bent over the front wheel, searching. Yes, there it was—the cut which had pierced right through the outer cover.

That puncture had been the real start of it all.

About half a dozen of us had cycled down to Mulstead Cove for a swim. In the early evening we were swishing along the tiny winding lane through Blackleigh woods on our way home. There was a sudden plop and my front tyre went down, hissing loudly.

The others pulled up too, and a circle of gloomy faces surrounded me. We were all hungry, longing for our tea. I felt absurdly apologetic, as if it were my fault some idiot had left glass on the road.

It was Mark who came to my rescue. "I'll mend it." Airily, he waved the others away. "There's no point in the rest of you waiting."

It seemed so generous of him, so gallant. Later, to my delight, he told me that he'd been glad to have the excuse to stay behind with me.

I had mended a puncture before, but I wasn't such a fool as to admit it. I sat on the bank and watched him, admiring his dexterity as he upended the bike and quickly slipped the inner tube out of the cover. With a contemptuous snort he had refused the basic repair kit I had fished out of the saddle bag, and fetched his own collection of tools.

"You really need a new tube," he said. "This one's just about had it. Still, I can patch it up for now."

Mark was only ten minutes doing it, and there seemed no valid reason to delay any longer. I stood up and took my bike from him, prepared to push off.

He hesitated, then as if overcoming an inner shyness, he said boldly, "Don't let's go yet, Jan."

I protested without conviction. "But shouldn't we be getting back?"

Mark threw himself down on to the grass bank. "I've earned a rest after all that hard work," he said with a grin. "Come on now, sit down again and don't argue." He patted the grass at his side.

I can't remember what it was we talked about. Everything in this world, I think, with all the earnest sense of discovery of adolescence. We talked until the daylight began to fade. I knew Aunt Frank wouldn't worry, but all the same . . .

Perhaps my restlessness showed, for Mark jumped to his feet. "I'm ravenous. Let's go into Sherbridge for some fish and chips."

Sherbridge was a good five miles away. "Yes, let's."

He put out a hand and pulled me up. We stood there looking at each other for several tense seconds, hesitant, uncertain. Then, almost angrily, Mark swung away and picked up the bikes.

But much later on, standing by Aunt Frank's gate in the dark, Mark found the courage to kiss me.

"Oh Jan," he whispered huskily. "You're so sweet. I think I'm falling in love with you. I hope you don't mind."

It was innocent of us to imagine we could hide our love from the gang. We were afraid of their jibes spoiling what was so precious to us. But in the event, they let us off quite gently.

Sally, bless her, was sympathetic but cautious. "You and Mark are pretty keen on one another, aren't you?"

It seemed a ludicrously mild description of the way we felt, but I didn't point this out.

"He's awfully nice," I admitted, blushing furiously.

Her plump kind face was made for laughter. The present anxious expression sat uneasily upon it.

"Yes, but then Mark's always been awfully nice. Jan . . . you won't let yourself get hurt, will you?"

I brushed this aside. "Of course not. Why should I?"

"Well, I mean . . . you're both very young, aren't you? At least, I suppose nearly eighteen's not really all that young for a girl, but for a man . . ."

She made no further attempt to warn me off. In fact, I believe that more than once when she knew Mark and I were off alone together she covered up for us to his mother.

Sally's brother Derek was already working in those days. Lionel Buxton owned a small factory making office furniture, and his nephew had joined the firm. In spite of being a little older than the rest of us, Derek still hung around with the gang when he could. But as the weeks passed we saw less and less of him. Someone discovered he had taken up with

18

a girl who was in the Sherbridge Repertory Company, and the boys pulled his leg about the affair crudely and without mercy. It was all meant in fun, but sometimes he would take their ribbing badly; and being in love myself then, I felt sorry for him.

We met him with Rhoda Lamont several times. That was inevitable because Sherbridge possessed only two coffee bars of the sort where young people hang out. On one occasion a crowd of us went to see the current play, Derek driving us rather grandly in his uncle's big Humber, lent for the evening.

Rhoda joined us afterwards for supper.

"How was I?" she asked, looking round at the boys. "Was I all right?"

They assured her she had been wonderful. It was a gross exaggeration. Her performance as the bullied younger sister of the heroine had been on the hammy side.

Rhoda took over the party, dominating it. She was certainly beautiful to look at— petite, with an impressive figure, a marvellous creamy complexion and long sleek raven-black hair. Daring make-up made her brown eyes look huge and luminous and provocative.

For some reason Sally, usually so ready to be friends with anyone, resented Rhoda fiercely. "The sex-kitten of Sherbridge," she sneered.

To me, Rhoda was rather alarming. Although only a little older, she always treated us girls like infants. I was in awe of her sophistication. She quite obviously had a vital sort of sex-appeal, and I would see the boys eyeing her surreptitiously— even Mark. Afterwards, I would spend a night of despair, before Mark succeeded in convincing me that his love was unchanged.

Although I met Mark's mother several times at the Buxtons', he seemed reluctant to take me into his home. But just once that summer there was a supper party at *Elgin House*. I had the feeling that Mrs. Galbraith was grudgingly extending what she regarded as the minimum acceptable hospitality to her son's friends.

Beautifully turned out in wine-coloured silk, her silvery-blonde hair piled high, she had looked like a queen. She welcomed her son's guests with gracious condescension, instead of the warmth and enthusiasm her sister-in-law, Mrs. Buxton, would have shown. We all felt constrained, unable to relax in her overpowering presence. Mark looked unhappy all the evening, and I felt desperately unhappy for him. He must have been acutely conscious that everyone was comparing his elegant home unfavourably with the comfortable, free and easy open-house of the Buxtons.

Some time during that party Mrs. Galbraith found an opportunity to single me out and have a little chat. It was neatly done. There was no acknowledgement of my friendship with Mark, but she carefully worked round to her son's cleverness, his ambitions, the wonderful openings ahead, his determination to get right to the top. It was a none-too-gentle warning that nothing must be allowed to interfere with her plans for him, certainly not his getting entangled with a girl at the very outset.

Feeling subdued, I asked Mark next day, when we were lying on the sands after bathing, "Are you really as clever as your mother says?"

He giggled. "Me? Didn't you know, I'm brilliant? I shall probably end up

Chancellor of the Exchequer, or something." Then he rolled over and kissed
me, and I felt I was in heaven again.

One glorious day I spent sailing with
Mark and his father in Weymouth Bay. I
knew Mr. Galbraith kept a small boat in
Mulstead Cove—Mark had pointed it out
to me when we had been there swimming,
but there had never been any question of
our using it.

I was surprised when Mark invited me
to join them one Sunday.

"Did your mother ask me?" I shot at
him.

He hedged. "Dad said it would be
okay." But he knew perfectly well he
hadn't answered the question in my mind.
"Mother never goes sailing nowadays," he
added. "She used to, often, but somehow
she doesn't seem to think it's quite . . .
the thing."

He hadn't meant to sound critical, I
know, but he was unable to conceal
his disappointment in her. I got the
impression that Mrs. Galbraith had
become too grand to be known to muck
about in a small boat.

I remembered that day's sailing vividly.

There was a stiffish breeze and the water was choppy, but the skill of the two men rapidly dispelled any anxiety I felt. Mr. Galbraith quite happily accepted me as a crew member, and showed remarkable patience with my clumsiness and complete ignorance of nautical terms. I took to him at once, but then I suppose that was inevitable, for he was an older version of his son. Both of them had the same absolute integrity, and the same carefree attitude to life which they almost certainly exaggerated a little to conceal a very serious purpose underneath.

At the time I only knew that Roland Galbraith was an architect in Sherbridge. Mark mentioned quite casually one day that his father was designing a concert hall for a booming midland industrial town, which had decided it could afford to go in for a bit of culture. That was how Mark put it, covering his pride in his father with a lighthearted aside.

I had been thrilled about this, and I remember saying to Mr. Galbraith how exciting it would be for him to look at the concert hall in future years and know that he was the creator.

His wide, friendly grin mocked any possible idea that his words were sanctimonious.

"I suppose so. But then I get a big kick out of seeing the houses I've designed. Somewhere for people to live in happily is the most rewarding thing for an architect."

I was already working in Kutain when the news broke in the national press of the opening of the revolutionary new concert hall. It caused quite a sensation, and brought Roland Galbraith instant fame, and soon afterwards, a knighthood. But he had little chance to take the retrospective pride in his work I'd imagined. Little more than a year later, his heart let him down, and he was enough of a name by then for the newspapers to report his death, too.

I'd lost touch with Bishop's Cranford news by that time. Aunt Frank was a most unreliable correspondent. I expect Mother's letters to her were bright, newsy accounts of the goings-on in Kutain, with plenty of irrelevant detail. My aunt's replies were erratic and very brief. She didn't mean to be unfriendly, I knew that.

24

But she couldn't imagine that anyone would be interested in local gossip.

For a long while after that holiday in Dorset I kept up a furious exchange of girlish confidences with Sally Buxton. Pages of glowing descriptions about life at our respective colleges, the exciting discoveries of the adult world. And I told her too about my boy friends, Mark's successors. I soon noticed, however, that Sally wrote almost exclusively of a certain Paul Andrews. It hardly surprised me that in due course, and without undue excitement, she married him. I had always known that when the time came it would be easy for Sally to fall in love with the right man and settle down to contented married life.

Our correspondence dwindled after that —our situations were so markedly different. But one of her last letters brought me surprising news. It had been added as a postscript, perhaps to soften the effect.

By the way, Mark got married last month to—guess who? Derek's ex girl friend Rhoda Lamont!!! A very quiet do up in London, and none of us invited! He's still at University, of course, so they've taken a flat. Fancy having her in the family! Still, thank heaven for small mercies—at least she's not my sister-in-law!

I was over the pain of loving Mark by then, but illogically it hurt that he had married young after all, not waiting to complete his University course. With bitter amusement, I wondered what his high-and-mighty mother had made of this. And it hurt too that he had married Rhoda. Why couldn't it have been someone I had never met?

I was still standing there in the garden, foolishly holding on to the rusty old bike as if it were made of precious metal, when I heard Mrs. Bird trilling from the cottage.

"Would you like a cup of tea, Miss Janice? I've got a pot on the go."

I was to discover that Mrs. Bird had several "pots on the go" each afternoon she came here. She could get away with that sort of thing at Mead Cottage. Aunt Frank could be relied upon not to remember when the last cup had been made. Was it half an hour, or three hours ago?

Carefully I put the bike back in the shed, and piled the tools around it again. That bicycle had too many memories for comfort.

I gave a lot of thought that afternoon to what I should wear at the Buxtons'. I told myself I wanted to make a good impression on these people who had only known me as a rather gauche girl. But I knew in reality I would be putting on a suit of armour, a façade to protect me from my innocent youth.

Even when I went up to my tiny, white-painted bedroom to get ready, I was still undecided. I opened the door of the heavy oak wardrobe, and took out the three possible dresses, laying them out on the patchwork bedspread. In the end, still very hesitant, I chose one of wild silk, in kingfisher blue.

How much had Mark told Rhoda about me? She must have seen for herself that summer how keen he and I had been on one another. But had Mark filled in the details? How much does a man tell his wife about past loves? Rhoda may have known all there was to know. Perhaps she and Mark had laughed together about such a tender young love.

Somehow it seemed important not to let myself down, so I took enormous pains with my appearance. I remembered that Rhoda had tended to overdo make-up, and I found myself using a careful minimum to achieve the result I wanted. I brushed out my dark hair and slipped on a headband matching the dress. I decided I looked quite good.

An odd thought struck me as I went down the steep, boxed-in stairs. Aunt Frank was waiting for me in the sitting-room, using the odd minutes making notes on one of the scribbling pads that were always scattered everywhere around the house.

She looked up and smiled. "Ready?"

"I've just realized you didn't mention Mark Galbraith's wife this afternoon," I said. "I suppose she'll be at the Buxtons' too?"

My aunt had already marched over to the door, but she swung round to face me again, surprised.

"Good lord! I suppose I took it for granted you would know."

"Know what?"

"Why, that Rhoda Galbraith was killed. It was just about a year ago—last May. She was on holiday in Brussels, and there was a fire in the hotel . . ."

I felt numbed with shock, appalled by the horror of the picture Aunt Frank's unemotionally precise words had conjured up. I felt the colour drain from my cheeks.

"Oh, but how awful! Poor Mark!"

My aunt didn't respond. Already she was lost again in her own private thoughts.

"F-blank-r-blank-blank-t-o-n," I heard her muttering. "Now what can I make of that?"

2

FIVE years had brought little change to Bishop's Cranford. It was still the same charming village with the thatched stone cottages in their small gardens, on either side of the road that gently wound up Blackleigh hill. Even the ginger airedale that lived in the house next to the "Wagon and Horses" was still there. The dog was fatter now and less nimble, but it still barked just as furiously as ever from behind the gate as we passed. A little further on I caught again the sweetly overpowering scent of honeysuckle that tumbled over the old stone wall of *Water's End*. I saw, however, that the cottage itself had been repainted, and a car stood in a new garage built on at the side. It looked as if the old man who used to sit in his porch, nodding and waving as we cycled past, had either died or gone away.

I turned to ask my aunt about him but checked myself, not wishing to disturb our companionable silence. I was used to Aunt

Frank and didn't mind one bit when she became lost in her own complicated chains of thought, locked and interlocked like the words in her crossword puzzles.

We must have looked an odd pair as we marched up the village street. Unlike me, Aunt Frank had made almost no concession to the social occasion. She had condescended to change her blouse to something softer than her usual tailored shirts, but the tweed skirt was the sort she always wore, and beneath it were thick stockings and stout brown brogues.

Used to Kutain where one hardly ever used one's legs except for dancing or tennis, I'd almost forgotten that Aunt Frank walked everywhere, scorning the car that for the most part stood idle in the garage. But at the last minute of getting ready I'd remembered and changed out of my dizzy-heeled sandals into something more amenable to a half mile walk. I couldn't come right down to earth on flat heels though, so I'd compromised. After all, you've got to *feel* right for cocktail drinking.

Abruptly, as though there had been no silence between us, Aunt Frank began to talk again. That troublesome space in the current crossword must have been neatly filled in. She could work like this, holding the complete frame of a puzzle in her mind.

"You'll be shocked when you see Lionel Buxton," she told me. "The poor man's a mere shadow of himself since he had that stroke last autumn. He's all there mentally —mercifully he never lost that. But Dolly has to wait on him hand and foot, and she's never able to leave him alone."

"How dreadful—for both of them!"

"Yes, it's been a bad time, but he does seem to be making progress at last. The doctor is very hopeful of a complete recovery. The main thing is that Lionel mustn't be allowed to worry about *anything*. It was worry that brought on his stroke in the first place."

"I see! What's happening about the factory, then? I suppose Derek is running it for him?"

Aunt Frank glanced at me, as if wondering how much to say. "Derek does a lot, of course, but somehow . . . I don't think he's quite got what it takes. If it wasn't for Mark . . ."

Maddeningly, she switched off again, and I couldn't decide how deliberate her withdrawal had been this time.

I'd concluded that Mark must be staying with his mother for a few days, but now it sounded as if he might be settled here in Bishop's Cranford. I just couldn't understand it. Why, with his qualifications as an economist, wasn't he holding down an executive job with one of the big industrial groups? Had Rhoda's death changed everything for him? Had he lost all his earlier drive and ambition? Did he feel that there was nothing left to strive for now?

The Buxtons lived in an ugly Victorian house standing rather imposingly in a lot of ground. It was kept neat in the front with clipped box hedges and bright flower beds, but the back, as I remembered it, was largely a wild shrubbery and orchard.

Two cars stood on the gravel outside the house, a red sports coupé and an immaculate black Wolseley. I wondered which was Mark's.

We crunched our way up to the front door. It was flung open to our ring and I was swept into a generous bosom and well and truly hugged.

"Jan dear! How lovely to see you again!" Mrs. Buxton thrust me back, the better to survey me. "My word, what a beauty you've become!"

Aunt Frank, completely at home here, disappeared into the sitting-room, leaving us alone. Mrs. Buxton went rattling on.

I looked at her excited kindly face, and realized she hadn't changed one bit. Her home reflected her personality—it was a battle of flowers. In the hall a rose-patterned carpet fought against the bright chintz curtains and the daisy loops on the wallpaper. A huge vase of mixed wall-flowers on a side table was sunk in this welter of colour. "I love flowers," Dolly Buxton would confide. It wasn't hard to believe. I think this exuberant display measured the prodigality of her heart.

"I wrote and told Sally you would be staying with Frank," she was saying. "She's going to try to come down for a weekend while you're here, but of course it's quite a long way from Worcester to bring a toddler."

I smiled. "How is Sally?"

"Oh, she's so happy with her Paul."

I asked after Mr. Buxton. "I was so sorry to hear about his illness."

Her eyes misted over for a moment, but she smiled at me bravely. "He's as well as can be expected, dear. Really he's made a wonderful recovery, when you come to think about it."

"It must have been a dreadfully worrying time for you."

"We must count our blessings, Jan dear. Lionel *is* getting better, slowly. He does so enjoy having people come to see him now he can't get out." She gave my arm a little squeeze. "He was quite excited about you coming. He was always very fond of you."

I suddenly felt a bit ashamed because the Buxtons had lately got left off my Christmas card list.

"Mr. Buxton was very kind to me, I know that," I said guiltily. "And so were you. It was wonderful the way you always made me so welcome here."

She sighed. "Those were happy days, weren't they, Jan?"

Mrs. Buxton sounded so wistful, and I couldn't blame her. Life must have seemed full indeed when Sally was always bringing home a crowd of young friends, the house noisy and throbbing with vitality. Now Sally was miles away in Worcester, and Mr. Buxton an invalid. Of course, she still had Derek, but he was not the gay companion his sister would have been.

I had slipped off my coat, and Mrs. Buxton hung it in the cupboard for me. "Come along in, dear. They'll be wondering where we've got to."

There were four people in the sitting-room, and Mark wasn't among them. I had so keyed myself up to meeting him again, that I couldn't hold back my flood of disappointment. I had to make a conscious effort to keep the smile on my face.

Aunt Frank was talking to the pathetically shrunken Mr. Buxton where he sat by the window in a low armchair. Derek was at a side table seeing to drinks, and Mark's mother, poised elegantly upon a high-backed chair, overlooked the scene disdainfully.

I felt Mrs. Buxton's hand on my arm, pulling me forward.

"You remember my husband's sister," she said, her eyes twinkling closely into mine. "*Lady* Galbraith."

It was a gentle hint that a slip on my part would come amiss. When I was here before, it had been plain *Mrs.* Galbraith.

I took my cue and spoke with formal politeness. "Good evening, Lady Galbraith."

She awarded me a gracious inclination of the head. But the eyes that surveyed me coldly were watchful.

"Ah yes. I believe I do remember you now. Didn't you visit us once with Sally?"

I was taken aback. I couldn't accept that she really had difficulty in recalling me—not after that little *tête-à-tête* at Mark's party. The sympathy I had been feeling towards her because she had lost her husband, evaporated instantly in face of this calculated insult. Why after all these years should she still bear me a grudge because I had threatened—as she thought —to upset her plans for Mark? How she must have hated Rhoda who had actually married him!

It was possible to detect a faint facial resemblance between Margaret Galbraith and Lionel Buxton, but there any likeness ended. He, when in normal health, was a good-natured family man. A little withdrawn perhaps, but nevertheless a man without any pretensions. His sister pretended to a great deal. She always had done, and now her aristocratic aspirations were reinforced with a title. It seemed to have gone to her head. She was dressed for the part and acting the part, so that she looked entirely out of place in the homely Buxton sitting-room.

Aunt Frank was deep in conversation with Mr. Buxton, but I saw he was watching me, a friendly smile on his face. I went over and took the feeble hand he held out.

Uneasy, tongue-tied for the moment, I propped myself against a small table by his chair. What did one say to a man struck down so savagely by illness? Should I avoid the subject or not? Mr. Buxton solved the problem by himself making the running, remembering my previous visit nostalgically, and saying nice things about my present appearance.

I asked him about Sally and her baby, and that struck the right note. He was obviously a proud grandfather, even though he was really only a great-uncle.

Mrs. Buxton had sat down beside Lady Galbraith, and I expect she found talking with her sister-in-law difficult. She joined herself to our conversation by calling across to me. "What do you think of that clever aunt of yours, Jan dear? She's become quite a personality on the radio since you were here last."

"Now don't pile it on, Dolly," said my aunt easily. "Just because I do a few quiz shows."

Derek had come across with a drink for me. "But it's true, Miss Prior, you *are* quite a personality. The whole village is proud of you. The landlord of the 'Wagon and Horses' has to make sure the radio is on in his bar when you're on the air, or he'd lose trade. They all want to hear you."

I smiled up at Derek. It was a very real pleasure for me to hear my aunt praised.

"I'm certainly going to make sure I don't miss the next show," I said firmly.

The older people reverted to their previous conversations, and I found Derek regarding me whimsically over his raised glass.

"Here's mud in your eye," he said, and tossed back the last of his sherry. He took a long and easy look at me, seeming to approve. "I see our little Jan's a big girl now—and very nice too!"

I might have remembered Derek as good looking if my standard of those earlier days hadn't been so utterly predetermined. For me, Mark had been the perfect man. I couldn't accept any sort of deviation from his husky, suntanned good looks, and his tousled fair hair.

Derek was dark and sleek—the immaculate sort of man chosen for hair-cream ads. Like his sister Sally, he was heftily built, though his height dispelled any suspicion of overweight.

He was very easy to talk to. Of course, those years in Kutain had trained me not only in small talk, but also in countering the light-hearted flirting with which men probe a girl's defences. I wasn't surprised when after only a few minutes he asked me to have dinner with him.

"What about tomorrow?" he said.

I was free as air, and I was feeling much too well to hang around doing nothing.

"Thank you, Derek. I'd like that."

As he fixed to pick me up, we heard a car outside the open window. I saw Lady Galbraith's eyes light up.

"That will be Mark," she announced.

I felt a sudden tightness in my chest. So, after all, I was going to see Mark this evening.

Derek jumped up to go to the front door, and straining my ears, I heard a muffled conversation in the hall. Then, unmistakably, came the familiar sound of Mark's throaty laugh.

I was caught off-balance, astonished by my own reaction. Before I could sort out my feelings, he appeared in the doorway.

It was the Mark I remembered. *My* Mark! For a second my heart stopped beating. Standing there at the door he looked more like a blond god than ever, but I noticed something else about him that hadn't been there before—an assurance, a new certainty.

He glanced swiftly round the room, smiling generally at the company. Just for a brief second he seemed to pause, and I felt his eyes resting on me. It was as if an electric current jumped the gap between us.

Mark strode over to Mrs. Buxton. "Sorry I'm late, Aunt Dolly. Old Henry Griffiths wanted to see me, and I couldn't refuse—not such a big customer."

He must have greeted his mother, he must have spoken to the others, but I was only conscious of Mark himself. My senses soaked up everything about him—the easy way he moved in his dark, well-cut suit, the resolute tilt of his head, the fair hair tumbling over his brow, the slight tenseness about the mouth that was his control over a sense of humour always too ready to laugh at life and himself.

Suddenly he was at my side.

"Jan! How wonderful to see you again!"

His nearness, the few words spoken into my ear, overwhelmed me. In that moment I was lost.

I was quite unprepared for the surge of emotion that swept through me like a forest fire. All that old love and longing for Mark, the adoration I had believed was submerged and drowned long ago, came rushing back. I had to struggle to tear my

42

eyes away from his deep blue ones, but I was scared he would see far too much. I dared not give any man such power over me—not even Mark.

I didn't trust my voice. Somehow I forced a light laugh.

"I was terribly sorry to hear you'd been ill," he went on. "I must say no-body would know—you look absolutely marvellous."

Obviously he expected me to say something. I'd always had enough to say for myself in the old days.

"I . . . I feel heaps better now. I collected some stupid tummy bug that made me allergic to the Kutain climate."

"Does that mean you'll be in England for good now?"

"Oh no. The doctor said a few weeks back home would put me right."

"And how do you like your exile in the Middle East?"

It was becoming easier to be natural. Mark always had a way of showing a strong personal interest in other people, and it worked even in my befuddled state.

"It's a very gay life out there," I said. "The European colony is very well organized—everything's laid on. But I admit the heat and dust and smell of oil everywhere gets a bit much sometimes. I've often longed for green fields and quiet country lanes."

He laughed. "You and I saw plenty of those when we cycled around together. Remember?"

Did I remember? But I only smiled. "I haven't cycled at all since then."

"You should, you know. It's wonderful exercise."

"No doubt you do it all the time?"

Mark grimaced at me, wrinkling up his nose. "We were talking about you," he said.

I wanted to go on with this casual, flippant conversation, but there was something I had to say. I had to say it now.

"Mark . . . I'm awfully sorry about Rhoda. I . . ."

The smile faded and I saw his lips tighten. "Yes, it was . . ."

Lady Galbraith interrupted us then, and perhaps it was just as well. She laid a possessive hand on Mark's arm.

"Did you remember to collect my watch from the jeweller's, darling?"

44

His smile came back. I never remember Mark getting impatient with his mother. He slipped a hand inside his jacket.

"Do you want it now?"

"Yes please. I feel so lost without it."

Mark took out the small jeweller's box, and his mother held up her wrist so that he had to fasten the watch for her.

"There," he said, like a magician performing a trick. "How's that?"

She frowned slightly, her lips petulant. "It's a little tight, dear."

He fixed the strap in another position.

Lady Galbraith was demonstrating to us all—but to me in particular—her son's devotion. A lesser man might well have objected, thinking a mother's domination would destroy his masculinity. But there was no question of Mark being dominated by his mother. Even as a girl I had been able to understand that the homage he paid to her was freely given, not extracted as a due.

A man with Mark's instinctive good manners could charm any woman. It was fortunate that his high standards and scruples prevented him from taking advantage of that fact. At least they had done, when I knew him before.

Lady Galbraith's interruption succeeded nicely in breaking up our conversation. After that the talk became general. I smiled and listened and chatted my way through the evening, trying not to let it become obvious that my eyes and attention were fixed on Mark. I suspect that his mother noticed. Although everyone else was being very nice to me, welcoming me amongst them again, Lady Galbraith ignored me to the point of rudeness. I could feel her hostility reaching and enveloping me like billows of smoke from a bonfire.

It wasn't until Aunt Frank and I were leaving that there was a chance to speak directly to Mark again.

"We must meet and talk about old times," he said.

"Yes, that would be nice." A sudden excitement flared with me. I wanted more than anything else to see Mark again, but I knew I'd be playing with fire. The force of my reaction to him had proved I was still far from well enough to have proper control over my emotions.

"That's fine," he said. "How about dinner tomorrow evening?"

"Oh, I'm sorry Mark, but I can't manage tomorrow." I hesitated. "As a matter of fact, I'm going out with Derek."

Again he made that so typical grimace, his nose wrinkling. But this time he didn't seem to be laughing.

"So Derek got in first? That serves me right for being late tonight."

I waited confidently for him to suggest the following evening, but he didn't. He shrugged. "I'll give you a ring, shall I?"

It was unsatisfactory—horribly unsatisfactory, but I had to leave it at that.

3

THE red sports car I had seen outside the Buxtons' belonged to Derek. He called for me the following evening, and we zoomed along the lanes I remembered so well from the saddle of my bicycle. Soon we were racing down the Sherbridge bypass, streaking past the slower traffic. I was used to fast driving out in Kutain, but there the dirt roads were long and straight and empty!

I couldn't entirely conceal my alarm, and Derek grinned.

"Don't worry, I know how to drive. This bus is good for a ton."

"I believe you," I said faintly.

After ten minutes or so, we pulled in at a roadhouse called the "Chequers", and Derek piloted me through the plush foyer straight to an alcove in the Tudor bar.

"I like it here," he said, leaning back against the dunlopillo cushioning. "A London firm took the place over a couple of years ago, and tarted it up a bit."

"Very nice," I said cautiously. I'd seen what he'd so carelessly paid the waiter for two drinks—extortionate even by Kutainian standards. I shuddered to think what our dinner was going to set him back.

"This is a very special occasion, Jan, so let's celebrate."

"What's so very special about tonight?"

He opened his eyes wide. "Need you ask? When I'm the envy of every man in the place?"

I could see the way the wind was blowing; I'd been taken out on evenings like this before. But I found I just couldn't respond to the mood. Thoughts of Mark were dominating the background.

"I was sorry to find your uncle was in such a bad way," I said soberly.

Derek's intimate smile vanished and he frowned into his glass.

"Yes, it has been rather grim, and all over nothing, really."

"Why, whatever do you mean by that?"

He shrugged. "He would worry so—just because we were going through a slight recession, like most other firms in the trade. But you know what Uncle

Lionel is—he works himself up about imaginary troubles . . ."

This was quite a new picture of Lionel Buxton to me. He had always struck me as such a placid man. I realized that my conceptions of all the Bishop's Cranford people were based on the impressions of a seventeen-year-old girl. I would have to be ready to revise my ideas.

"Mark is with the firm now, I gather?" Nothing more had been volunteered by Aunt Frank to explain Mark's presence here, and I longed to know all about it. I hadn't questioned her, thinking there would be a good opportunity to get the full story this evening.

Derek gave me a sharp look. "What's Mark been telling you?"

It sounded critical, and I rushed to Mark's defence. "Nothing, nothing at all. It was just something my aunt happened to mention."

Derek was fingering the stem of his glass, twirling it round and round so that in the end the liquid spilled over the edge. A hovering waiter rushed forward to mop up the drops at once.

"And what was it your aunt said?"

I watched my tongue. "Only that Mark is helping out in the business."

"Helping out?" Derek gave a short laugh. "I suppose Uncle Lionel thought two heads were better than one, and I don't like to . . . Oh, to hell with that, Jan. We're out to enjoy ourselves this evening." He got up quickly and reached for my hand. "Come on, let's go in and eat."

It was a marvellous dinner, and several times we danced on the tiny floor to the music of a three piece combo. But all the while my thoughts were drifting. I still didn't understand just how Mark fitted in to the set-up at Bishop's Cranford. Both Aunt Frank and Derek had seemed evasive. I badly wanted to know just what Mark was doing here, but I didn't like to declare my interest in him too positively by asking a lot of quesions.

I tried to forget about Mark—to push him out of my mind. After all, it was hardly fair to Derek. He was making a splash evening of it, and all I could contribute was to smile wanly across the table, and dance in a half-hearted fashion.

Zealously, I threw myself into the mood

of the occasion, and was rewarded with the discovery that Derek was a fabulous dancer. I began to enjoy myself as he led me expertly through a quick-step and cha-cha. Then they ran down the lights for a foxtrot, a sentimental oldie.

Dancing in the dark, I felt the arms around me tighten, pulling me closer . . .

Till the tune ends, we're dancing in the dark.

We moved in unison to the slow, throbbing, sensuous beat. I nestled against his shoulder, and dreamily glanced up through my lashes at the dark head bent over mine . . .

Dark head! If only it could have been a fair one!

My instinctive recoil was surely barely noticeable, but it was enough to make Derek frown. I cursed myself for a romantic fool. How could he help not being Mark?

There must have been dozens of girls around who would jump at the chance of this sort of night out with Derek. And here was I, dancing with him, eating his dinner and mooning about another man. It made me feel cheap.

Despite that frown, Derek took my odd behaviour very well. He certainly didn't once give up trying. When we drove home, much later, it wasn't the mad swoop of the outward journey. I found the red sports car could be driven at a leisurely pace as we trickled through the country lanes. I remembered my local geography well enough to realize that the detour we made "for a change" took us several miles out of our way.

Outside Aunt Frank's cottage we slid to a gentle stop. A crescent moon hung high over Bishop's Cranford, giving the deserted village a brushing of silver. There wasn't a light to be seen anywhere, except for the lamp that Aunt Frank had left on in the hall.

Derek turned to kiss me, and I was prepared to enjoy it.

"Jan, darling," he whispered, taking me into his arms. I tilted up my face until our lips met.

"It's been a lovely evening," I said as I drew back. "Thanks, Derek."

"But it isn't over yet," he murmured. His kiss, soft at first, grew more demanding; asking for, expecting a return.

I found I couldn't respond. I had nothing to give Derek.

"I'm out much too late," I said in a new voice, a voice of decision. "I'm supposed to be convalescing."

"In a minute," he said urgently. "Don't go in for a minute, darling."

It was a time for firmness. Before Derek realized what I was doing, I had slipped from his arms and out of the car. Then, with the door safely between us, because I liked him and wanted to show it, I leaned over and kissed him again, lightly. "Goodnight, Derek. Thanks for a wonderful evening."

Waving back to him, I skipped up the garden path and was inside the cottage in a flash. It was nearly a minute before I heard the car drive off.

Up in the tiny bedroom, stepping out of my dress, I congratulated myself that I had managed things rather well in the circumstances. It really had been an enjoyable evening. It wasn't Derek's fault that his kiss had meant so little, had awakened no response. It wasn't his fault that my mind refused to forget Mark.

I had believed that I was over Mark long

ago. Yet one short meeting in a room of people had destroyed that myth. Mark Galbraith filled my thoughts. He was the only man I wanted to kiss me now.

I decided that I had shown Derek quite definitely there couldn't be anything serious between us—and without hurting his feelings. I'd shown him we could only be friends. But when I had slipped into bed between the cool sheets, I lay there wondering. Who was I kidding? It wasn't difficult to imagine how Derek's mind might be working at the moment. My behaviour in those last few minutes could just as easily have given the impression that I was leading him on, playing hard to get. I could hardly have done a better job if I'd wanted to.

But in the morning I couldn't go on worrying about Derek. I found myself *living* for Mark's promised call. Surely he would phone today? I hovered over the telephone, willing it to ring.

I didn't have long to wait. A few minutes before eleven the phone bell jarred through me. I was so keyed up that the sound made me flinch. I leaped to answer it.

"Hallo, Jan darling."

It nearly had me fooled for a minute. The words I wanted so badly to hear tricked me into mistaking the voice.

"Are you there, Jan?" asked Derek anxiously.

I tried to cover my savage disappointment. Trying too hard, I talked a lot more than I should. "Hallo, Derek. Sorry to sound dumb, but you see . . . Aunt Frank was expecting a call. You took me by surprise."

Absurdly, I wanted him to get off the line. Mark might choose just this minute to ring me, and finding the line engaged . . . The very idea panicked me.

Derek seemed all set for a lengthy chat. "Tell me what you're doing right now," he said.

"Doing? Why, nothing in particular."

"I wish I could be with you," he murmured. "Jan, darling, can I see you again tonight?"

"No!" I cried. Then I attempted to soften my abruptness. "I really have been ill, Derek. The doc said I *must* take things easily."

"Well then," he said cheerfully. "I'll

have to be patient, won't I? How about tomorrow?"

In the end I think I made him believe I was too tired and weakened by my illness to make further plans for the time being. He sounded crestfallen, but he wouldn't give up easily.

"I'll ring tomorrow to see how you are," he said firmly.

I spent a day of frustration tied to the phone. I willed the wretched thing to ring. It was two days ago that Mark had promised to phone me, and he had done nothing about it. It must be that I had only imagined the spark passing between us. By now he had probably almost forgotten my existence.

Time dragged drearily by. Derek phoned again as promised, and again I stalled. But Mark didn't ring. I dared not go out. I hung over the telephone, and even when I sat outside in the sunshine I kept very near the open back door. Before the phone could ring twice I'd be there.

The bell was so silent that more than once I thought the phone must be out of order. I lifted the receiver and listened until the operator answered. Dismally I put the thing back, muttering apologies.

I was bitterly angry with myself for getting so pent up. If this was all the interest Mark had in me, I was letting myself down by getting into such a state about him. But whatever I told myself, I lived for his call, and for nothing else.

Fortunately Aunt Frank seemed not to notice, and we carried on with the casual routine of Mead Cottage. Some of the time my aunt shut herself away in her little study, but mostly she worked wherever she happened to be. She had a wonderful capacity for concentration, and could just switch off her attention from anything else.

Every day she read through several newspapers at a great lick. You could almost see her sifting the facts and stowing them neatly into her filing cabinet of a brain—to be brought out later, no doubt, in the form of brilliantly accurate answers to difficult quiz questions. Over breakfast she would polish off a few crosswords at breakneck speed, writing in the answers almost as quickly as she read the clues.

"Must watch my rivals," she would say with a grin.

Meals tended to be erratic at Mead Cottage. As often as not Aunt Frank seemed to forget all about eating, and then hurriedly looked round to see what she had in the house. If it wasn't for Mrs. Bird, who on her afternoons arrived loaded with useful stores, and departed leaving a casserole in the oven, I think Aunt Frank would have lived largely on bacon and eggs and bread and cheese.

Mrs. Bird was new since my previous visit. She was a small, spritely woman, and it was almost as if her married name had dominated her personality. Her habit of cocking her head to one side reminded one irresistibly of a sparrow.

She loved to chatter too, and welcomed my presence as an audience. Obviously, she didn't know what to make of Aunt Frank's detachment, but seemed to accept eccentricity as befitting a celebrity.

"Very exciting it is to listen to Miss Prior on the wireless. Of course, I can't really understand what it is they're on about, but it's wonderful the way she answers all those difficult questions. She knows all about lots of things you and I would never even think about."

It was lucky that Mrs. Bird's interest in keeping the cottage clean and moderately tidy didn't depend upon Aunt Frank appreciating her efforts.

"Some lovely things, your aunt's got— all those antiques! But she hardly so much as looks at them. Not like Her Ladyship —now she knows exactly what she's got, and everything has to be spick and span for her."

"Her Ladyship?" I had pricked up my ears.

"Yes, I mean Lady Galbraith. I work for her in the mornings—every day, Monday to Friday. It's a big house, you see, and she insists on its being kept just so."

"Yes, I know. I . . . I went there once to a party."

"When you were here before? That would have been before Sir Roland died— and Mr. Mark's wife, too?"

"Yes."

"Sad, weren't it? Two deaths in the family so close together. I wonder when the third will be, that's what I say. Of course, you have to be ready for it with someone a bit older like Sir Roland was—even though it were sudden with a heart attack. But for a young woman like Mrs. Mark . . ." She shook her head. "Real tragic!"

I couldn't help myself asking, "I suppose you met her?"

Mrs. Bird nodded. "Just the once. She came down with Mr. Mark for the weekend soon after they were married. I didn't actually meet her to talk to like, but I saw her arrive. Beautiful, she was—I've never seen anyone so lovely. To think her young life was cut off so short! Poor Mr. Mark! His heart must have been broken."

I didn't want to hear any more and changed the subject rapidly by offering to hoover down the stairs. Actually, I quite enjoyed helping a bit in the house. It was a novelty for me, because in Kutain it wasn't the done thing for the British community to lift a finger. You could hardly move about the house without falling over the army of servants. Anyway, I had nothing else to do here at Bishop's Cranford, while I waited for the phone to ring.

In the afternoon, two days after my evening out with Derek, Aunt Frank announced she was off to post her "copy" to the *Sunday Globe*, and thought she would drop in at the Buxtons' at the same time. She asked me if I'd like to go with her.

I was reluctant. But it was a lovely afternoon, and I had no good reason for refusing. Not one I could tell my aunt, that is. Anyway, I was beginning to feel a weak fool, hanging around like this for a man—any man. I decided to go.

Mr. Buxton was having a nap, so we three women made a tour of the garden. It brought back memories for me, but it was sad to see such signs of neglect.

The tended flower beds and trimmed grass extended no further than was immediately visible from the front of the house. The kitchen garden, once flourishing with trim rows of vegetables and crisp saladings, had now been abandoned. The pleasantly wild shrubbery and old orchard I remembered were now sheer overgrown wilderness.

Mrs. Buxton surveyed it sadly, apologetically. "I'm afraid we've had to let it go since Lionel's been ill. I do try to do what I can, but I haven't much time. Fortunately old Williams still comes in once a week and manages to keep the front looking respectable."

We talked about plants, and Aunt Frank seized on new names with interest. I knew she had no enthusiasm for flowers. Her business was with words, and she took a good look at every new one that crossed her path.

"How do you spell it, Dolly?" she asked sharply.

"K-N-I-P-H-O-F-I-A. It's usually called Red Hot Poker. Of course, this isn't a very good specimen."

Aunt Frank nodded, considering. If she thought it might come in useful some time, she would store the name away in her mind. If not, out it would go, ruthlessly.

Faintly we heard the tinkling of a little bell.

"Lionel's awake," said Mrs. Buxton, leading the way back to the house. "Let's go in and have a cup of tea."

Her idea of a "cup of tea" was generous to a fault. That I knew from the days when a crowd of us could count on a hearty spread, whenever we turned up at the house. I followed her to the big old-fashioned kitchen, while Aunt Frank went in to the invalid.

Dolly Buxton's voice flowed on as we prepared the feast.

"Frank's been marvellous, you know, dear. Poor Lionel gets so bored just sitting there day after day, but she always manages to liven him up. Some days she'll play chess with him by the hour. It makes a nice change from that constant TV."

I was putting the lid back on a cake tin, thinking a slice of fruit cake would do us very well. But Mrs. Buxton wouldn't allow such a mean spread.

"You'll find a chocolate sponge in the round tin, dear, and there are some jam tarts left. Do you think I should just make a few cucumber sandwiches?"

I managed to steer her off that. "I'll bet Aunt Frank's a wizard at chess?"

She nodded, sighing. "I do wish *I* was. Lionel does enjoy it so. I know the moves of the various pieces, but I get so muddled when I start to play."

Laughing, I said, "I'm not much good

at chess, either. I think it demands the more logical mind of a man . . ."

"And that's just what Frank's got!" She checked herself. "Of course, I didn't mean that in an unkind way . . ."

"But it's quite true, and I'm sure Aunt Frank would take it as a compliment."

Mrs. Buxton fetched cups and saucers, and put them out on a tray. "I've got so much to be grateful to Frank for. I know how busy she is, but she manages to find time to come here and keep poor Lionel amused. I don't know what I'd have done without her help, really I don't."

"You know you can always count on me," I told her. "As I said, I'm no good at chess, but I'd be happy to sit with Mr. Buxton if you want to go out. I've plenty of time to spare."

"It's sweet of you to offer, Jan, and I'll remember if I'm stuck. But at your age you should be out enjoying yourself." The friendly eyes crinkled significantly as she looked straight at me. "I gather you and Derek had a nice evening out together! He has seemed very pleased with life since then."

It was as I had feared. Derek was

reading too much into what had happened when we parted. Altogether too much. Partly to cover my embarrassment I went on to talk about the firm.

"It was a good thing Derek was there to run the factory when his uncle was taken ill so suddenly."

She had turned away from me to make the tea. The boiling kettle was in her hands but she put it down again on the stove. "Yes," she said slowly, "it was very lucky. It's all been such a worry. Derek's a good boy, of course . . . but frankly, if it hadn't been for Mark I don't know what we should have done."

This was my chance to get more information.

"I rather gathered Mark is working for the firm now. I must admit I was surprised. I mean . . . I imagined he'd have a job in London."

"He did have, dear. He was doing very well at International Machinery by all accounts. But when we were so desperate, with the doctor warning me what any more worry would do to Lionel—well, I was prepared to try *anything*. I knew it was asking a lot, but I *did* ask Mark, and he gave up everything and came here like a shot."

It was so like Mark. His consideration for other people went beyond the normal bounds. But I wondered what his mother thought of him giving up what must have been a career glittering with promise. Or was she just glad to have him back within her province?

"And are things better for the firm now?" I asked tentatively.

"Oh, much! Mark really has worked wonders—he's just full of ideas for developing new lines. Lionel's delighted about it. He says getting Mark to come in was the best thing we ever did."

I'm sure Mrs. Buxton didn't realize that with every word of praise for Mark, she was denigrating Derek. It was Derek who had expected to take over the factory. I remembered hearing him boast that one day the business would be his. But whatever the exact set-up was now, whichever of the men might be the titular head, it was clear enough who was at the helm. No wonder Derek had not wished to discuss Mark's part in the firm.

I wanted to hear more about Rhoda's

death, but I didn't need to prompt Mrs. Buxton. She soon got around to it.

"Such a horrible death! Wasn't it dreadful?"

I nodded soberly. "They couldn't have been married long when she . . ."

"Hardly more than four months. I felt so sorry for Mark. The poor boy had to go over to Belgium to identify the body." She shuddered, then lowering her voice to a confidential level, she went on, "Mind you though, I can't pretend I was ever much taken with Rhoda. The once or twice she came here with Derek she was always . . . well, never just natural and friendly like the rest of you young folk."

"Still," I said, "she was very beautiful. I remember the rest of us girls envying her for that."

Mrs. Buxton agreed. "Yes, Rhoda certainly had the looks. Actually, Jan, she was rather like you. Quite a striking resemblance, really, in the face."

I gave a half-laugh. "Come now, Mrs. Buxton, I wasn't asking for compliments."

"No, but I'm serious. As a matter of fact . . ." She again took up the kettle, which had been boiling merrily for several minutes. "As a matter of fact, I've often wondered if it wasn't because she was so reminiscent of you to look at that Mark . . ."

She stopped. I waited, breathless.

"Oh, darn it!" she said. "There won't be enough water now. I'll have to put on another lot."

Soon after breakfast next morning I took the bus into Sherbridge. I made myself go out, determined not to allow my life to be dominated any longer by a yearned-for phone call.

The quaint old town had a charm I'd never forgotten. Industry had hardly touched it. In fact Buxton's Office Furniture, small by most standards, was still the biggest factory in the place.

But I didn't go near Buxton's. I steered clear, walking slowly up the ancient High Street. A tourist guide would have drawn my attention specifically to the Town Hall by Nash, the Norman Church with its square tower, the three-hundred-year-old almshouses "for needy spinsters of respectable habit". These things were certainly very noteworthy, but I preferred to soak

69

up the general atmosphere. Sherbridge had adapted to the twentieth century craftily, almost painlessly, by the simple means of building a by-pass road around itself. The endless traffic roared past two miles away, and Sherbridge dreamed on . . .

I was dreaming too. Tired after a morning's strolling, I waited outside the station for a bus back to Bishop's Cranford. Across the road was the little repertory theatre where Rhoda used to work.

A car glided to a stop beside me.

"Going home?" Mark was smiling up at me. "Jump in quick. I mustn't stop here or I'll have the bobby after me."

If I'd had any warning of Mark's approach, it is possible I could have controlled my fierce reaction. As it was, I almost fell against the car, my legs weak and trembling, my heart already pounding. I made an awful mess of getting in, catching my coat in the door, and slamming it three times before the lock caught. I felt an utter fool.

"That was lucky," Mark said as he drove off. "Seeing you, I mean."

I managed to find my voice. "How come

you're going back to Bishop's Cranford at this time of day?"

"Pure chance." He turned to me momentarily, and grinned. "Or rather, kind fate. Mother's car is laid up, and she has some committee meeting or other in Sherbridge this afternoon. I really can't spare the time, but I promised her I'd go home for lunch and bring her back with me."

The journey was only just over five miles. It certainly wouldn't take more than fifteen minutes at the very most. I longed for it to go on and on.

I made myself talk naturally. "Your aunt's been telling me how you came to the rescue of the firm."

He jerked his head slightly, as if flicking away any credit that might have attached to him. "It's lucky that I was able to come. I expect Aunt Dolly explained how vital it was that Uncle Lionel shouldn't be worried in any way. He seemed to be caught up in a vicious spiral—his ill-health meant he couldn't give proper attention to the business, and the consequent running down of the firm made him worse. Finally, the strain of it all brought on the stroke."

71

I nodded. "But I gather things are going better now?"

"Well, I think the worst will soon be over, touch wood!"

"Touch wood?" I echoed. "I'll bet the improvement is due more to your hard work than any luck."

The old Mark shone through; the boyish grin I remembered so vividly. "Thanks for them kind words, lady."

He was silent for a moment, perhaps because a crossroads demanded his attention. Then quite suddenly he said, "I was terribly glad when I heard you were coming to stay with your aunt, Jan. I've been looking forward to seeing you again. What about you?"

"Well, as a matter of fact . . ." I stopped in confusion. How could I explain that I had thought Mark was still a married man? That I'd come here knowing nothing about Rhoda's death?

"As a matter of fact—what?" he prompted me.

"Well, you see . . . I didn't really expect to meet up with you at all. I thought of you as working in London." I tried to be flippant. "Carving a career for yourself, you know."

"You did think of me then? That's the main thing."

I said nothing.

Mark went on, "All that getting to the top stuff, Jan! I remember how I used to spout about Sherbridge being too small to hold me. Life doesn't always turn out the way you expect, does it?"

I glanced at him quickly, and saw that his smile had a sadness about it.

"And what about you, Jan? Have all your dreams come true?"

"I'm not sure I had any dreams," I lied. "But it's a wonderful life out in Kutain. Everything a girl could want."

It was true, really. At any rate, as true as most things are. But I hadn't realized out in Kutain that life was hollow, meaningless—without Mark. I'd forgotten the ecstasy his nearness would bring. I had thought my life was pretty complete. And if sometimes I'd briefly envied other girls who had married and settled down happily, I'd argued that my time would come. When I was ready for it, I would find happiness in marriage, too.

"Everything?" Mark said, repeating my own word.

I looked down, understanding what he was getting at, fearful of giving too much away.

"Does that mean you've found . . . love?"

"No!" I cried, so quickly that it sounded like a protest. Trying to dispel that impression, I made my words light as air. "I'm in no hurry for that."

There was silence between us again. Mark turned the car off the main road, down the lane to the village. There was such a short way to go now.

"How did you enjoy going out with Derek?" His words came out suddenly, as if he'd been rehearsing them over in his mind.

"It was fun. He took me to the 'Chequers'—you know, that place out on the by-pass?"

"I know it." He didn't sound very approving.

We were coming into Bishop's Cranford now. Mark turned off by the church.

"Drop me on the corner," I said. "I expect you're in a hurry."

He didn't seem to hear me, driving on until we reached Mead Cottage. He stopped at the gate and turned to me.

"I've been meaning to ring you to fix something up," he said slowly. "But these last few days have been like crazy at the office. Even worse than usual."

"Oh, that's all right, Mark," I assured him brightly.

And then he came out with it, the invitation I had been longing for these past days.

"Can you manage Sunday? I thought of taking the boat out—the weather seems to be set fair. Do you feel like a day's sailing?"

"Oh Mark, I'd love it!" I hadn't meant to sound quite so wildly enthusiastic, but now it was said I didn't care. "I haven't been sailing for years. Not since . . ."

"That's fine, then. I'll pick you up here on Sunday morning—about ten-thirty suit you?" He reached across and opened the door. "And thanks, Jan."

Him thanking me! If Mark only knew the wild joy I felt at the prospect of a whole day with him.

My heart was singing as I bounced into

the cottage like a child home from school, swinging my handbag as if it were a satchel. It was lucky for me that Aunt Frank was so blind about some things.

4

THERE was an open space alongside the jetty where Mark could park the car. Tufts of coarse grass grew between the granite blocks, rustling in the brisk sea breeze.

There was remarkably little sign of life. A cluster of cottages, brightly lime-washed in pink and pale blue and white, and a tiny pub. Some lobster pots were drawn up on the narrow pebble beach, looking forlornly abandoned. Out on the sparkling water, protected by the wooden jetty, rode a few small sailing boats, perhaps twenty in all.

As we unloaded tackle from the car, Mark sniffed the air.

"Couldn't be better," he pronounced. "The wind's just right."

"Oh Mark," I cried in delight as I looked around me. "It's all just as I remembered it. Nothing seems to have changed."

"We have, Jan. We're both five years

older. But maybe that's a good thing. We were so terribly young before."

There didn't seem anything to say to that, so I went on looking down at the water.

"Can you pick out the *Shamrock?*" Mark asked me.

"You've still got the same boat then?" I was searching hastily, not wanting to slip up.

"Sure. Dad kept her on when I went up to University. After he died she was a bit neglected, of course . . . But I've got her in good trim again."

The lines of one craft seemed familiar. I gulped, and took a plunge.

"Is that the *Shamrock* alongside the black and white boat?"

His quick smile told me I was right. "You must have a good eye, Jan."

We had arranged nothing about food for our lunch, so I'd taken a chance and prepared a picnic. Mark had a look in the box.

"Yum, yum," he said, poking around. "Chicken, sausage rolls, grapes. You *have* done us proud. And you remembered the beer—good girl! I was planning on scrounging some cheese rolls out of George Evans at the 'Smugglers' Arms' over there."

We scrambled aboard, and Mark handed me a bright yellow life jacket.

"This is new, isn't it?" I asked. "I don't remember wearing one of these before."

"It's the done thing nowadays—like crash helmets on motor bikes."

It was a curious sensation wearing the padded garment. "I do feel a podge," I said, laughing. "So this is what it's like to be fat."

"You still look pretty gorgeous to me," he said, with meaning in his eye.

I stowed away the picnic box, covering it with a waterproof to make sure we weren't reduced to eating soggy pastry. Then I asked Mark what I could do to help.

"You can hold this halyard," he said, throwing me a rope. A string of instructions followed, and I was kept busy trying to work out what he meant.

We cast off and edged gently into the wind. Then up went the mainsail. It filled with a clap, and we were away at a spanking pace, heading out into the open bay. Only when the sails were trimmed did we have time to talk.

"Do you come sailing much?" I asked.

"Most Sundays. I like to get away from it all once a week." Because that sounded a bit serious, Mark grinned, as he always used to. He never could bear to be thought pompous.

"You can manage the *Shamrock* alone then?" I was fishing, of course. I hoped not too blatantly.

He patted the tiller. "The old girl's as meek as a lamb, though naturally it's easier with someone to crew for you. Derek came out with me once or twice when I first came back, but I don't think he was too keen somehow."

"No, he's not really the outdoor type, is he?"

The mention of Derek cooled me down for a minute. I'd managed to stall him off so far on the grounds that I mustn't get overtired. But how could I use that excuse again, when he got to hear I'd been out all day in the boat with Mark?

Life gets so *complicated* sometimes, and it could be so wonderfully simple!

Far out in the bay, after a good hour's

sailing, we hove to. Down came the canvas, and we rode gently on a long swell.

"I'm starving," Mark announced.

I got out the food. "I brought along enough for four," I said. "Remembering how you used to eat like a horse."

"I still do!" He added modestly, "A very well-bred horse, of course."

He punctured the two cans and poured the fizzing beer into paper cups. We lounged back, wriggling into comfortable positions, and ate. And I was happy.

"You make a good crew, Jan love," Mark said out of the blue.

I blushed. *Me!*

"My father thought so too. You remember that time you came out with us? He told me afterwards what a thoroughly sensible girl you were."

"He was a nice man," I said, delighted that I had earned his approval. "So friendly, and easy to get on with." And then I wondered if it sounded like a back-handed criticism of Mark's mother. She'd made it so patently clear that she did not approve of me, either then or now. In a way I could sympathize with this attitude before, when I'd been a kid of seventeen

81

and might well have tempted Mark into ruining a promising career. But why now? Why should she be so set against me?

I concluded that Lady Galbraith probably disliked on sight any girl Mark might show an interest in. She'd lost him once, and fate had handed him back to her. Even her brother's illness played into her hands, because it had brought Mark back to live under her very roof.

Mark said something, and I jumped to attention.

"Sorry, I was dreaming."

"Funny little Jan," he said, smiling oddly. "That's an old trick of yours, going off into daydreams. What was this one about, eh?"

"Oh, nothing. Nothing special."

He was leaning against the backboard, one arm still lying idly over the tiller. I was propped lower down, the other side from him. Not much space separated us.

Mark leaned forward, bending until his face was barely a foot from mine. "I've often thought of you," he whispered.

". . . have you, Mark?"

He bent over still further, the smile gone, his blue eyes serious. His cheek brushed my hair. I heard him catch his breath, and then his lips were full on mine. It was as though the time since we had parted was swept away. I knew again a joy I had known before—a fierce joy I had forgotten.

I yearned for his arms around me, holding me close. My own hands reached up as if governed by a will of their own, wanting to caress the springing fair hair . . .

Mark moved back, and the magical moment was gone.

"Hey, the wind's rising! We'd better get nearer shore." He scrambled to haul the mainsail.

To me it seemed like the same steady breeze.

When the evening chill came down we sailed back along the coast and into the little harbour. Leaving the car where it was, we strolled up the steep slope to the tiny inn.

"The landlord's wife will knock us up some bacon and eggs, if that will do?" said Mark.

"It sounds wonderful."

We sat outside the little pub on an old

oak bench, and chatted to some of the locals as we drank a glass of beer. Then we were invited to go through to the kitchen at the back where a huge supper had been prepared for us.

Neither of us spoke much on the drive home through dark, silent lanes—little country roads that were once so familiar to a pair of young cyclists. I was happier that evening than I had ever been in all my life, wanting nothing more than for this to go on for ever . . .

When we got back we stood for a moment by Aunt Frank's garden gate. Mark took me into his arms and kissed me.

"Oh Jan, my dear sweet Jan," he murmured.

It was quite a time before at last he released me.

"It's been so perfect," he said, taking my two hands together and pressing them between his. "I want to see you tomorrow and tomorrow and every single day, but I'm so hellishly involved with work. There's nothing I can do about it, darling, with Uncle Lionel so ill."

"Don't worry, Mark," I said. "Don't let

it worry you." I felt so gloriously confident of his love now. I could afford not to be greedy for his time.

But it wasn't easy to be patient when Mark was away from me. Our infrequent meetings were glorious fleeting moments, separated by dragging intervals filled with longing. I knew very well that Mark saw me as often as he possibly could, but jealously I begrudged every hour of the evenings he spent at his office.

If I'd had a job to do, something to occupy my mind during at least part of each day, I might have avoided this absolute preoccupation with Mark. As it was, the circumstances that had brought me here conspired against me. I thought of Mark and longed for Mark every hour of every day.

I went up the Buxtons' house quite often. It was the least I could do by way of repayment for all the kindness they had shown me in the past. And in any case I enjoyed their company.

Mr. Buxton was touchingly grateful to have someone to talk to. I didn't attempt to play chess with him, having an idea that my feeble efforts would be likely to make him more ill than to act as a therapy. Sensibly we settled for draughts, and I suppose because he was half contemptuous of such a simple game, I was able to sneak in a good move often enough to keep my end up.

It was inevitable that I met Derek there occasionally, which always seemed to please Mrs. Buxton. Sometimes I suspected that she was deliberately delaying my departure until he got home. If Aunt Frank wasn't with me, Derek would then take me back to Mead Cottage. It became more and more difficult to evade his pressing invitations.

Once he challenged me directly. "Why are you avoiding me, Jan?"

"But I'm not avoiding you, Derek. It's just . . . it's just that I'm supposed to be convalescing . . ."

He cut in angrily. "That doesn't prevent you going around with Mark, I notice. You go running to him if he so much as lifts a finger. What's wrong with me, for God's sake?"

It was an impossible question to answer. I did my floundering best. "I'm sorry

Derek. It's just that . . . well, I do like you very much, but . . ."

"You always were soft about Mark, weren't you?" His face darkened, and he gave a harsh laugh. "I don't know what you girls see in him."

"I'm sorry, Derek," I said again, rather desperately. "I . . . I can't help the way I feel . . ."

"Fancy carrying a torch for the man all these years," he sneered. "And where do you think such sweet devotion is going to get you?"

"I . . . I don't know, Derek." Even in my own private thoughts I hadn't dared look too far into the future. Happiness in the here and now was all I lived for.

Derek was still arguing when we reached Mead Cottage. His parting shot was particularly painful.

"It doesn't look as if Mark was faithful to *you*, does it? He soon got himself hitched. Are you happy knowing you would be his second choice?" I was silent at that, and he persisted. "Well, are you Jan?"

Derek's words came back to me during my solitary hours. Jealousy about Rhoda was something I had to fight. The plain fact was that Mark had loved another woman enough to marry her. But Rhoda was dead. Surely it was possible for a man to fall in love again—and another love need not be a lesser love. But whether that was true or not, I was so helplessly in love myself that I was prepared to accept whatever kind of love Mark was able to give me.

Mark never spoke about Rhoda. Once or twice I had mentioned her, bringing her name into the conversation. I was always careful, anxious not to wound. But Mark steered straight away from the slightest reference. I sensed that he just didn't want to talk about her. Outwardly he appeared to have got over the shock of Rhoda's tragic death, but I couldn't know what scars had been left on his heart.

The little time we had together was always happy, full of our old kidding gaiety. Each Sunday we spent the day sailing, and whenever he could manage to be free in the evening, we would go to the cinema in Sherbridge, or drive to Weybridge or Swanage for dinner. Mark always showed great affection and tenderness, but somehow I got the feeling he was holding himself back—deliberately not getting too deeply involved with me. Gradually, I began to notice that all our talk was of the past or the immediate present—never of the future. He gave no sign of being disturbed about my impending return to Kutain.

Was this muted love affair no more to Mark than a repetition of our teen-age romance? Did he regard it as no more than a charming and amusing interlude?

I remembered our half-flippant, half-serious conversation the day he'd driven me home from Sherbridge. "Had I found love?" he'd asked me. *"I'm in no hurry for that!"* Why had I said it? Mark could hardly be blamed for supposing that I was ready for another flirtation without strings.

When nearly six of my eight weeks were up and Mark had still made no move to bring matters to a head, I could only conclude that marriage just wasn't in his mind. Perhaps Rhoda's sudden death was still too near for him to consider taking another wife in her place.

If only time wasn't so short. If only I hadn't to go back to the Middle East in a couple of weeks. It looked as if once again I would lose my chance of happiness with Mark because the time wasn't right.

Until now Aunt Frank's blindness, her complete lack of interest in my love life had been very convenient. I shuddered to imagine what Mother would have been like at this stage—her over-enthusiastic pushing us together, her conversation liberally sprinkled with arch raillery and innuendo. Poor Mother! I loved her dearly —and I was glad she was far away in Kutain.

But there is a happy medium in all things. Right now I could well have done with more perception on Aunt Frank's part. How I would have welcomed a suggestion from her that I might care to extend my stay with her.

The ironic thing was that she wouldn't mind at all my staying longer than planned. I knew she liked having me. Aunt Frank was far too straightforward ever to dissemble. "I shall miss you when you've gone, Jan dear," she had said more than once. Now, if she said it again, I would almost be tempted to ask if I could stay on a bit.

Wild ideas flitted through my mind that I might pretend to have a sudden relapse. But one look in the mirror was enough to show me I couldn't hope to get away with that. Just as Mother had prophesied, I was already quite completely recovered. There was no possible health reason why I shouldn't go home any time now.

I was seeing so pitifully little of Mark. He seemed more and more involved with the factory, though he said very little to me about the business. I didn't press him. It was perfectly understandable that he wanted to turn his back on work for a few hours when he could, and I was only too thankful that I could help him relax.

Most of what I knew about the factory I had learned from Mr. Buxton himself. He often talked to me about his business when he tired of our draughts games.

Derek had told me that his uncle's worries about the firm were largely imaginary. I couldn't judge whether Mr. Buxton was in fact exaggerating them in his mind, but it was quite clear from what he said, and the little Mark did tell me, that the firm had indeed been facing a crisis. For some years, apparently, competition from the big manufacturers had been fierce. A small firm like Buxtons' was undercut on price, and found their established customers slipping away one by one.

"I don't mind telling you, Jan, that at the time I had my stroke, I saw no way out of our difficulties," Mr. Buxton confided. "But Mark came along full of new ideas. We owe him more than I can say."

I gathered that Mark had launched out into new fields—office furniture tailored for the individual customer; complete filing systems; loose-leaf records in a brand new form. Such ideas were eminently suitable for a small firm whose adaptability to meet special requirements had the edge on big firms mass-producing standard lines. At last things were beginning to look up. But it called for tremendous effort both to reorganize the factory and find new markets at one and the same time.

There was a new problem Mr. Buxton didn't know about. His secretary, who was in her late thirties and had been with the firm since leaving school, had suddenly announced rather breathlessly to Mark that she was going to get married.

"We dare not let Lionel know," Mrs. Buxton told me. "He'd be so upset. Of course, it means even more work on poor Mark's shoulders, until he can train another girl. In a small place like this there's little chance of finding a competent secretary—they tend to stay with the same firm until they get married, like Mary has done."

Curiously, the great idea didn't hit me until the following evening. Where could Mark possibly find a good secretary around here who wasn't already in a job?

He didn't have far to look!

This was no time for false modesty. I was a darned good secretary. After all, I *should* be—considering my parents had spared no expense on my training. On top of that, I'd had experience in a slick modern commercial organization where initiative and tact were in constant demand.

Aunt Frank would be delighted with any idea that promised help to the Buxtons in such a practical way. And I believed Mark would be thankful if I offered myself as a stopgap. I could stay on long enough to see him through this very difficult spell, long enough to train another secretary into the ways of the firm. And long enough, I hoped, to become indispensable to Mark in another way . . .

Anglo-Kutainian Oil were jolly good employers, and I knew they'd willingly grant me unpaid leave. Mother, being Mother, would inevitably scent romance in the air, but she was too far off to do anything about it.

I made up my mind to raise the matter with Mark when I saw him the next day. If, as I expected, he was pleased with the suggestion, then I would stay on at Bishop's Cranford as long as possible, and pray that time would bring the answer I craved for. If Mark refused my offer then at least I would know where I stood. I would know that he didn't want our relationship prolonged, that there was no future between us.

I was alone in the cottage that evening. Aunt Frank had gone off to Bristol for the first of a new series of quiz shows, and would be away for the night. The Buxtons had asked me to go to their house and listen to the programme with them. But I had refused. I made an excuse about wanting to wash my hair, and said I'd listen-in at the cottage. I didn't want to risk another argument with Derek. He had never given up, and knowing my aunt was away, he might be even more persistent when he escorted me home.

I wandered around the cottage singing to myself, happy now that I'd found some action I could take. The weather had turned to rain in the afternoon, and it was pouring down outside, beating against the windows in little flurries. Already by eight o'clock it was so dark that I put on the lights and drew the curtains to make the room cosy. Felix had sprawled himself on the hearthrug, pretending there was a fire in the grate.

I settled down to listen to the quiz.

Aunt Frank came over the air exactly as she was in the flesh, succinct and definite, quite sure of herself when it came to solid, knowable facts. I could understand her popularity, because she emerged as a real personality. Despite her erudition, there was no hint of conceit about her. The warmth and sympathy of her elusive character shone through. I could imagine listeners saying to one another, "That

Frank Prior—she's so clever, and yet not a bit of side about her."

Later on I was sitting with the radio turned right down, listening to one of those programmes of records for "squares". Not that I'm a square, but anyone can enjoy a good Irving Berlin number.

Above the strings I heard a sharp grating noise, and realized that someone was walking up the path. My thoughts passed quickly through hope (could it be Mark?) to alarm (was it Derek?). Then the speed and lightness of the footsteps told me it was not a man. A neighbour, I expected.

When I opened the door I saw a young woman in a white raincoat, tightly belted, a matching hat pulled down over her long hair. She carried a big shoulder bag on a strap.

I didn't recognize her. "I'm afraid Miss Prior is away," I said, standing back so she could step in out of the rain. "Can *I* help you?"

She came right in and rather unexpectedly shut the door behind her.

"But it's you I have come to see."

"Me?"

She laughed. "Yes Jan. Don't you know who I am?"

The pinkish light from the shaded wall-lamp wasn't very strong. I looked again at her rain-spotted face, looked more closely.

"I'm awfully sorry," I said. "Your face is certainly a bit familiar, but I'm afraid I just can't quite place you . . ."

Again that laugh. It was rather husky, and uneasy memories stirred in me.

"It was a long time ago, Jan, and we've both changed. I wouldn't have recognized you either, if I hadn't known . . ." She stood there, grinning at my perplexity.

"I'm sorry," I said again. "But I can't . . ."

"I've been hearing tales about you, Jan. They say you're casting big eyes at my husband. I can't allow that you know."

As she spoke she slipped off her white hat, and shook out her long black hair. The gesture was characteristic. That faint half-recognition clicked in my mind. I hadn't any doubt now who this girl was.

"Rhoda!" I whispered, reaching back for support from the wall. "But it can't be . . ."

5

"**W**ELL? Aren't you going to ask me to sit down, Jan?"

My legs were jelly. Somehow I managed to falter my way into the sitting-room and slump into a chair. Rhoda followed me. Numbly I watched as she peeled off her wet mac and carelessly dropped it on the floor. She arranged herself comfortably on the upholstered settle, kicking her shoes off and putting up her feet.

At last I found my voice, though it came out as the feeblest croak. "But I don't understand . . ."

"You thought I was dead?" She curled her lips in amusement. "Oh Jan, how very convenient that would be for everyone concerned, if only it were true. But as you can see for yourself, here I am, large as life and twice as natural."

"But . . ." I said stupidly, searching for words. "But the fire in the hotel in Brussels . . . ?"

"We . . . I managed to get out in time. Nobody noticed in all the excitement."

She had lit a cigarette, and now leaned back, thoroughly enjoying the shock she had caused me.

I sat there trembling. My hands were cold and clammy, my chest felt as if it would burst. I couldn't believe this was really happening. I had to fight to hold back my tears, to conceal my agony. Rhoda, by announcing her existence, had in a single moment destroyed all my dreams. And she was enjoying it! A malicious smile hovered on her cruelly beautiful face. She was like a vicious little girl who takes pleasure in toppling another child's carefully built up tower of bricks. I didn't yet understand how or why Rhoda had turned up after being supposed dead for over a year. But instinctively, I knew without any doubt at all that her intentions were evil. She had deliberately stayed away all this time because it suited her. She had only returned now for her own selfish reasons.

I gave full vent to the anger that surged within me.

"How *could* you have done this to

Mark? Letting him believe you were dead? How could you?"

Negligently, she flicked ash on to the turkey rug.

"Because it happened to suit me very well to disappear at that moment."

"But Mark was your husband! Think of what it must have done to him to get news of your death."

"I imagine it cheered the poor goof up no end. It would have been a happy release for him."

The way she talked about Mark made me want to get up and hit her. I did stand up, and she must have guessed something of what was in my mind.

"My, my," she taunted me, flickering her long dark eyelashes. "You have got it bad. I mustn't say rude things about your lover-boy, eh? But then you see he's mine, really, isn't he? So I've got a right to talk about him any way I please. You haven't got any rights at all—not as far as Mark is concerned."

In a way Rhoda's mockery did me good. It helped me to pull myself together. I went over to the radio, to switch off the smooth flow of syrupy music. I swung round on Rhoda.

"Why have you come back? Why come to me?"

She nodded approvingly. "That's more like it—now we can get down to brass tacks. It all looks very simple to me. You want Mark, and he just happens to be *my* husband. It seems to me that if we're sensible about it we ought to be able to do a deal—a deal that would suit us both."

Rhoda was looking at me brightly, as though she expected to be applauded for her cleverness.

"I don't know what on earth you're talking about," I said. But I did. It sickened me, but I knew all right. And she knew I knew.

"I'd better put you in the picture," she said. "It doesn't look as if Mark has told you much. He and I were all washed up from the beginning. Mind you, strictly as a man, I had no complaints. But you can't live on sex alone, Jan—however much you might think you can, the way you are about him now."

"You can keep your beastly insinuations to yourself," I shouted.

She stared at me in pretended surprise. "You're not telling me it's all platonic between you two? Not in this day and age?"

"If you've come here merely to insult me, you'd better get out." But I didn't mean her to go. Now she'd started, I had to hear her to the end.

"Don't get so excited, Jan," she said, very much amused. She lit another cigarette, eyeing me closely over the lighter flame. "Of course, Mark would be quite a good catch for a girl nowadays. I hear he's gone into the family business, and that things are picking up for Buxton's. It shouldn't be long before the money begins to roll in. But when I married Mark, he hadn't got started—he was still just a student living on an allowance from Papa. And that didn't go far! I soon got pretty chuckered with always being so hard up and never going anywhere, because Mark had to study all the time. It wasn't at all what I'd bargained for."

"And what had you bargained for?" I asked scornfully. "You must have known how it would be—getting married before Mark had finished his training."

Rhoda shrugged. "Oh well, we all make mistakes! I'd know better now, that's for sure. But how was I to guess it would work out like it did when his father died?"

"I suppose you thought Mark would inherit a lot of money because his father was famous?"

"There wasn't any money—or anything else . . ."

I didn't see that this line of conversation was getting us anywhere.

"Look here," I told her sharply. "Don't beat about the bush. Say what you've come to say."

Nothing I said seemed to rile her. She just went on smiling steadily as if she was genuinely amused.

"I walked out on him in the end, you know."

"Walked out on him? But Mark never said . . ."

"No, I don't suppose he did. It must have suited him down to the ground, thinking I'd died in that fire. That is, if he *did* think so."

"But of course he did! Mark went to Belgium and . . . and identified your . . . the . . . body."

"Did he now?" Her laugh tinkled. "Well then, whoever's body he saw, it certainly wasn't mine."

"But . . . but what were you doing in Brussels? I thought you'd gone there on holiday . . ."

She tossed back her black hair and laughed again. "It sounds to me as if that Mark of ours is pretty good at spinning a tale. Holiday be damned! I'd run off and left him, I tell you. Run off with another man, if you want to know."

There was silence for a moment. Then, spitting out the words, Rhoda said, "Oh, you needn't look so high and mighty. Life's been easy for you. I've had to do the best I could for myself."

"And you thought leaving Mark was the best thing?"

"Yes, it was," she said defiantly. "Best for him as well as for me. I told you, we were all washed up."

My brain wasn't functioning properly. I still couldn't understand.

"But if you'd decided to leave Mark, why all this business about being killed in a hotel fire?"

"Oh that! Well, you see, the fire was a

stroke of luck. Poor old Bill—that's the chap I was with—thought he had covered his tracks. But then he found they were on to him, after all. He had to disappear in rather a hurry. The fire came at exactly the right moment. We grabbed at the chance and . . . and 'died'."

I looked at her with contempt. "You mean to say you left Mark to run off with a . . . miserable little crook?"

"Bill was okay—just a bit unlucky, that's all. There are plenty of respectable business men in the City who've done what he did—and worse."

"And now I suppose you've left this man?"

She regarded me sorrowfully. "Oh sweetie, I would hardly turn up again if I was still with Bill, would I? As a matter of fact, we broke up about three months back, after the cash ran out."

"Three months ago! And what kept you from bothering Mark all that time? A guilty conscience?"

She wasn't in the least put out by my insulting remark. "Actually, it never occurred to me to look up Mark again. I soon found someone to take Bill's place, but it didn't work out too well. He wasn't up to much, and we lived in a scruffy little dump in the Barrows. He'd only got a few hundred quid he'd come in to."

"Which you kindly helped him to spend, I've no doubt. And now it's gone, you've ditched him?"

"Right first time! Give the lady a prize!"

I'd never liked Rhoda when I'd met her before, but I hadn't then imagined that she was capable of such ruthlessness. To her, a man was merely something to be used, to be picked up and then tossed away like an old glove when his usefulness was over. I wondered whether Mark had ever realized what she was really like? Or had he loved her too much to see the rottenness behind her mask of beauty? Perhaps even now, in spite of what she had done to him, he would rejoice to know that she was still alive. The idea made me ache with jealousy.

"Why have you turned up now?" I asked again. "Surely you don't imagine Mark would take you back after this?"

But Rhoda was still his wife. She was the only woman who had any claim on him, and Mark might want it that way.

Rhoda was rippling with laughter. "Be your age, Jan. Can you see me settling in this dreary little hole?"

"What is it you want, then? Why have you come here?"

"I've come to prevent a nasty scandal. After all, think of the complications if I turned up again."

"Do you mean you'd try to black-mail . . . ?" I was horrified. "But Mark wouldn't . . ."

"No, I don't think he would. But her Ladyship, his dear mother, she'd pay up all right. She'd do anything to prevent the murky past coming out. Actually, I was originally going straight to the old girl— I'd have enjoyed that. But now I've got a better plan. You see, Jan, I made a few enquiries first, just to see how the land lay —it's really marvellous what you can pick up in a village pub. I heard all about young Mark Galbraith going around with some girl, and how it looked as if wedding bells weren't far off. Of course, I didn't catch on at first—not until somebody mentioned that the girl was staying with her aunt, Miss Prior. And then I remem-bered how keen you'd been on Mark in the old days. So I thought I'd trot along to see you."

"Just what are you hinting at, Rhoda? You'd better come straight to the point."

"All right, here it is, then. Mark thinks I'm dead, and wants to marry you. I suggest you make it worth my while to clear off and never be heard of again."

"You must be crazy," I burst out.

"Why?" she asked, and I'm sure she meant it. She couldn't see anything wrong with her preposterous suggestion. "It boils down to this, Jan. You want something—I've got it. Okay then. What do you offer me for Mark?"

"This is ridiculous," I cried out. "Mark and I aren't even engaged . . ."

"Don't play the little innocent with me, Jan. Maybe Mark hasn't actually asked you yet, but you'll not let it lie there. A girl can always find ways of . . . encouraging a man. She can always make herself indispensable to him."

My face flamed. Only a few minutes before Rhoda had arrived, I'd been planning to do just that—make myself indispensable to Mark. My furious blush didn't escape Rhoda.

She grinned at me. "Hit the nail on the head, did I? Come on now, what am I bid for this virile specimen of manhood?"

"You really believe I'd bargain with you over Mark?" I flared.

"Whyever not? Anyway, I'm only asking a thousand for him."

"A thousand pounds! You must be raving mad!"

"Don't try to kid me, Jan. I seem to remember that daddy's in the oil business. We all know what that means in the way of lovely lolly."

I was staring at her dumbly, unable to believe my ears.

She shrugged. "I might be willing to drop a bit if you're hard up. Say seven-fifty. There, that's my last offer."

"You disgust me. I wouldn't do any sort of deal with you—not even if you'd clear right out of our lives for sixpence."

Rhoda lifted her legs off the settle with a lazy movement, and stretched, sighing in satisfaction. She bent over and slipped on her wet shoes.

"You'll change your mind when you've cooled off, Jan. If you've got any sense, you will. Seven hundred and fifty pounds for the exclusive rights to a man like Mark —attractive, and clever with it. Why, Jan, it's a snip."

I was filled with loathing for her. I watched, not speaking, while she strolled over to where she had dropped her raincoat on the floor. She shook it out with distaste, the drops spattering around. Without hurry she put it on, fixing the belt tight into her slim waist. She pulled the hat down over her head.

"God!" she exclaimed. "What I need is a nice hot bath! I'm going to stay at the 'Wagon and Horses' tonight, so you can let me know tomorrow how soon you'll be able to pass over the cash."

"I'll never pay you a single penny!" I hissed. "*Never!*"

She had gone out to the front door. As I watched from the sitting-room, she turned, her hand on the latch.

"You're not as stupid as you pretend, Jan," she said easily. "You'll pay up. I'm not worried."

And then she was gone. The door slammed after her, and I could hear her footsteps clicking lightly down the path. The gate banged and there was silence, except for the monotonous drumming of the rain.

I dropped down into a chair, and my anger gave way to hopeless despair. Tears rolled down my cheeks, tumbling faster and faster. Great sobs rose in my throat, choking me, shaking my whole body with their intensity. I had never known such misery before.

Had the horror of the last hour really happened? Surely it must have been a ghastly nightmare, and soon I would wake in my bedroom upstairs?

But I knew it had been no nightmare.

The smoke of Rhoda's cigarettes still hung on the air, pungent and unfamiliar in Mead Cottage. And over by the settle a dark damp patch on the carpet confirmed her visit only too plainly.

6

THE rain was still beating down steadily outside. My storm of weeping had played itself out, leaving me sick and ill and fit for nothing —an empty shell, drained of emotion.

With an effort I pulled myself together and tried to think. But all the thinking in the world couldn't avoid the one unassailable fact that everything was over between Mark and me. Over before it had truly started. I had to accept the stark cold reality. I had to reconcile myself to returning to the Middle East in a couple of weeks time. Kutain seemed to me nothing more than a hot, arid desert now. Anywhere in the world would seem like a desert without Mark.

And what about Mark himself? What would Rhoda's return mean to him? He must have loved her once. Could love ever die so completely that a man would actually welcome his wife's death in such tragic circumstances? Was it possible that Mark had rejoiced in Rhoda's apparent death?

That was what Rhoda had suggested, but I couldn't bring myself to believe it.

But if he had loved her, and mourned over her, wouldn't he be overwhelmed with happiness that she had been restored to him? As for her deception, it's so often said that love is all forgiving.

Perhaps even now he would want Rhoda back.

I might have been able to bear it if Rhoda had loved Mark, if she was sorry for what she had done. But I knew she cared nothing for him; she had returned only to make trouble.

I was tortured with doubts as to what I should do with the knowledge that Rhoda was still alive.

My instinct was to warn Mark. Wasn't it better that he should learn the truth from me? I loved him, while Rhoda only meant him harm. I had no doubt that he would learn about her sooner or later. Either directly, or if Rhoda reverted to her original blackmailing scheme, then through his mother. Whichever way it was, the shock to Mark would be devastating. Rhoda would choose her own time, a time to suit herself. She would spare no thought for Mark's feelings.

I knew I *had* to tell Mark that Rhoda was still alive. I had to tell him now, immediately, before it was too late.

The appalling problem was *how* to do it. If I admitted to seeing Rhoda, I would have to explain the outrageous reason for her visit. How could I tell Mark that, according to village gossip, he and I were well on the way towards marriage?

There seemed to be only one way out. Somehow I must make Mark believe that I had undeniable knowledge that Rhoda was still alive. If I could make Mark think that this information had reached me through some third person, then perhaps he wouldn't question me too closely. Perhaps I wouldn't have to admit that Rhoda had come to see me.

Before I had time to see any possible objections to this plan, I reached for the phone and asked for the Galbraith number. It was ten o'clock. I hoped Mark was home by now.

The receiver was lifted at the other end, and my heart sank as I heard the precise voice of Lady Galbraith.

"Bishop's Cranford four-three."

I forced myself to speak in a matter-of-fact tone. "Good evening, Lady Galbraith. Could I speak to Mark, please? Janice Prior here."

Her measured words nicely conveyed the distaste she had always shown for me. "I'm afraid my son is not home yet. Is there something I can do for you?"

"No, nothing thank you. But I would be grateful if you'd ask Mark to ring me when he comes in . . ."

"I will tell him. But it is not likely he will be home early enough to ring you tonight."

My control broke a little. "Oh, it doesn't matter how late he is. It's very important for me to talk to him right away, so if you wouldn't mind . . ."

"Very well," she said coldly. "I will give him your message."

It was clear Mark's mother was not pleased that I should be phoning him. It was even more apparent she thought it utterly unreasonable that I expected him to ring me back whatever time he came in. I was left with a thwarted feeling, not at all sure that my message would be delivered.

As the minutes ticked slowly by, I paced up and down the small room impatiently. I went through to the kitchen and put on the kettle to make myself a cup of tea. I tried reading, but even the newspaper was more than I could take in. I would read the same lines through again and again until the print became blurred.

Old Felix gave me something to do. He came mewing for his nightly saucer of milk, and as I put it down I tickled him behind a silky ear. He purred loudly, his tail held straight up like a mast. I remembered that Rhoda had reached out idly as the cat passed her, and stroked him. Felix had reacted in just the same way as with me, delighted to be fondled. It didn't matter to him who did it.

"Oh puss," I said, as he lapped up the milk. "How I envy you! As long as you have somewhere warm to sleep, regular feeds, and someone to talk to you, that's all you need."

It was past one o'clock when I woke up. I was sitting awkwardly in the big armchair, my neck stiff. Felix was a warm soft bundle on my lap. I put him down gently on the carpet, and he hardly stirred.

116

Could I have slept through Mark's phone call? I was sure it wasn't possible—the phone was there on the table, hardly a yard from my ear. It was clear enough that Lady Galbraith had not bothered to pass on my message.

Could I ring Mark now? But it was so late. My call would no doubt disturb Lady Galbraith, and she would want to know why I was ringing him up in the small hours.

Inexpressibly weary, I dragged myself upstairs, flung off my clothes, and crawled into bed, not even bothering to wash.

In the morning the sky was heavy and grey, though the rain had stopped. I woke feeling I was late for something, but I couldn't pin it down. The sensation only lasted a few seconds, then the memory of what had occurred came crashing down on me, flattening my spirits as a heavy storm flattens the grass.

Dismally, I looked at the clock. It was twenty-to-nine.

Mark would be leaving for the office any minute. I jumped out of bed and ran down to the phone. Fortunately, it was he who answered this time.

"Hallo, Jan!" He sounded surprised.

"Mark!" I cried urgently. "I tried to get you last night. I left a message with your mother."

"Sorry, darling. She was already in bed when I got home, and she's not up yet. What's the matter, Jan? Is something wrong?"

I didn't want to alarm him on the phone. But how could I bring him to the cottage at this hour of the day?

Speaking very carefully and precisely, trying not to allow the slightest falter to betray my agitation, I asked him to come round and see me.

"Do you mean *now?*"

"Yes please, Mark. I'm sorry to bother you, but something has come up that's rather important."

It was obvious that I hadn't succeeded in playing it lightly. Mark's anxiety was only too plain.

"Jan, what is it? Are you all right?"

"I'm perfectly all right. It's just . . . well, come round on your way to the factory, and I'll tell you about it."

"I was on the point of leaving, Jan. I'll be with you in five minutes."

There was barely time to dress myself and run a comb through my hair before I heard his car draw up outside. I ran to the door, then stopped, and opened it slowly, unhurried.

He looked at me, one swift glance. "Jan, whatever's happened?"

My appearance had given me away. Anguish had left its scars. What was the use of pretending? Mark knew perfectly well that I was terribly distressed.

I led the way into the sitting-room, and then turned to face him squarely.

"Last night I had some unexpected news. It will be a shock for you, Mark."

"What is it, Jan darling?" Mark came forward and took hold of my shoulders, but I slipped away. If I let him touch me now, I might say too much. I might tell him *all* the truth.

"Mark," I said, "Listen to me . . ." And then I dried up, looking at him foolishly.

"Jan, for God's sake! Something awful's happened, hasn't it?" He came to me again, and put his arms round me so that I couldn't escape him this time. He held me like that, quite roughly. "Tell me! Come on now, tell me!"

"Rhoda . . ." I said in a low voice.

I felt his reaction. His whole body seemed to jerk. "*What* did you say? *Rhoda?*"

"Yes, Mark!" I cried desperately. "I've got to tell you. Rhoda is alive. I . . . I *know* she is."

"No!" he shouted. "No, you don't realize what you're saying. It . . . it isn't possible." He thrust me aside, and strode over to the window. He stood there with his back to me, staring out. Then he turned slowly, facing me again, the width of the room between us. Every vestige of colour had drained from his face. For a moment I thought he was going to faint.

"How . . . how do you know?"

"I was told . . . Oh, it's true, Mark. I *know* it's true."

He bent his head down turning his face away again, whispering so I could hardly hear. "This is what I feared would happen."

His words staggered me. "But Mark, you told everyone . . ."

" . . . that she was dead? Yes, I know

I did. And I believed it. I did believe it, Jan, only . . . I was never absolutely certain."

"What do you mean? Surely you saw her . . . body?"

His voice was bitter. "Have you ever seen the body of someone burned to death? How could I be sure? I looked at the charred remains, and I felt sick. It was *supposed* to be Rhoda—they told me it must be her. And I said, yes, it was, because I just wanted to get away, and forget . . . But afterwards I could never feel positive."

He slumped down on a chair, and looked up at me, his eyes pleading for understanding. "You see, Jan, the way it happened, her death appeared to be a tragic loss for me. I didn't have to explain to anybody that our marriage had been a failure—an utter farce." He looked down at the carpet, and again I could hardly hear his words. "Rhoda had already left me. She had run away with another man."

So Mark had known she had gone to another man. Had Rhoda thrown it into his face? I could believe it of her. I could believe almost anything of her.

Mark added in a tired, flat voice, "Marriage with me didn't turn out as she had expected."

I ached with pity for him. "Did you love her very much?"

"Love? What do we mean by love? I was infatuated with her and I succumbed —a university student doesn't often have a beautiful woman like Rhoda for the taking. And after that, it wasn't difficult for her to play on my sense of decency."

"But I don't understand."

He looked at me with a sort of yearning. "No, Jan, you wouldn't understand a mind like Rhoda's. She used the oldest trick in the book. She said she was pregnant. And then, when we were safely married, she announced that it had been a false alarm."

"Oh, Mark!"

"But she soon regretted marrying me. She realized her mistake when my father died."

"You mean she thought you would inherit a lot of money from him?"

"Perhaps she did. But oddly enough that wasn't the main thing for Rhoda."

"What was it, then?"

His eyes were looking far away, back into the past. And what he was seeing caused him pain. "Rhoda didn't love me. I don't think she was . . . is . . . capable of loving anyone. She just wanted a husband. She could have married Derek, but for some reason she suddenly seemed to think I was a better proposition. It was just after Dad got his knighthood and looked all set for fame and fortune . . ."

"But you said it wasn't so much a matter of money."

"Don't you see, Jan? I was Sir Roland Galbraith's son. Rhoda had it all worked out in her mind that when Dad died, she, as my wife, would become Lady Galbraith. She didn't appreciate the difference between a Knighthood and Baronetcy. I didn't inherit the title, of course, and Rhoda was bitterly angry." He shuddered. "We had a horrible scene that night. And soon afterwards she left me."

"Oh, how could she!"

"To be honest, it was a relief to me when she went off. But I knew that sooner or later the news would reach Bishop's Cranford. And I knew too how upset Mother would be when it became public knowledge. Poor Mother! She can't help it—she just can't stand the least hint of scandal."

Rhoda had used those words! She may have been ignorant about many things, but she had certainly summed up the weakness of Mark's mother.

"At first I stalled and told our friends that Rhoda had gone on holiday," Mark went on. "And then, before I needed to invent another story, came the news of that hotel fire. The authorities in Brussels seemed so certain that the body they showed me was Rhoda's, and I just agreed with them. Ever since then, people have supposed I've been heartbroken over Rhoda's death, and I thought it was best to leave it like that." He shook his head in a lost sort of way. "I thought it almost certain that she was killed in that fire, but there's always been this slight doubt in my mind. Lately, I've been haunted by a feeling that she might have been alive— lying low somewhere. That's why . . ."

He stopped, and I waited in silence.

"Up to now," he began again, hesitantly. "Up to these last few weeks I didn't care much whether or not I was free to marry again . . ."

A flame leaped in my heart. "And now you do?" I whispered.

There was love and pain in his eyes. "You know that, Jan darling. Surely you know it?"

I couldn't help the sigh of relief that escaped me. "I wasn't sure," I murmured. But the flame in my heart had died down. It was too late now.

Mark stood up and came to me. He caught me by the shoulders. "As soon as I saw you that evening at the Buxtons', I *knew*. It was the same all over again—I was just as desperately in love with you as ever. You felt it too, Jan, didn't you? Tell me!"

"Oh Mark, my darling, of course I love you. But you didn't say anything, and I was going home so soon . . ."

"I've been wretchedly unfair to you, Jan, I know that, but . . ."

"I do understand, Mark."

The relief of knowing at last that he loved me, and wanted me as I wanted him; the stress of the last few weeks when I hadn't understood; the anxiety of the hours since that awful scene with Rhoda —it all caught up with me. I broke down. I was desolate, without hope.

Mark's arms were all at once gentle. He held me closely to him, stroking my hair, soothing me. "Darling, please don't cry."

At length he said quietly, "You haven't explained how you came to hear about Rhoda. Who told you, darling?"

Now that I knew he loved me I was able to tell him. I couldn't go on hiding the real truth.

"She . . . she came here, Mark. She came to see me last night."

"Rhoda was *here?* In the village? Good God! But why did she come to you? What on earth is she up to?"

Miserably, I told him the whole horrible story. As he listened, his face darkened with anger.

"She expected you to buy her off for a thousand pounds? It's monstrous . . . !" He groaned. "Oh Jan, I'm so desperately sorry that you should have been dragged into this."

We stood there clinging to one another. It was as if we both knew that when we parted this time, it would be for ever.

"I'll have to see her, Jan. I'll have to have it out with her. Did she tell you where she is living?"

"She said she would be staying at the 'Wagon and Horses' last night. She told me to get in touch with her there if I changed my mind."

"I'd better go there now. I must see her right away."

"What will you say to her, Mark?"

"I'll tell her . . . I'll tell her . . ." His hands fell to his side in a helpless gesture. "I don't know, Jan . . ."

He stood hesitating, and I realized that never before had I seen Mark so much at a loss. It was clear that here was a situation he was unable to grasp firmly and act upon. Mark was a man of action. Indecision must have lain heavy on him.

At last he turned away and opened the front door.

"You'll come back, Mark? You'll let me know what happens?"

"Yes, Jan. I'll be back," he promised.

It was a tiny glimmer of comfort in the darkness of my despair.

7

THESE last few weeks I had spent so much of my time waiting for Mark. I had been waiting for him to tell me that he loved me, despairing that he ever would. Now it was very different. I knew that Mark felt about me as I felt about him. There was nothing hidden between us. What I had longed for so desperately had come about, but in circumstances I could never have imagined.

As I settled down to wait for Mark again, hope had all gone. I had no idea how long he would be. My tortured mind tried to follow him, to picture what would take place between Mark and his wife.

Rhoda might not even be up yet. Perhaps at this moment Mark was cooling his heels in the pub lounge, awaiting her pleasure. He could hardly go up to her bedroom without admitting who she was. Not in a small village like Bishop's Cranford! It suddenly occurred to me that we didn't know what name Rhoda had registered under. It would certainly cause eyebrows to be raised at the "Wagon and Horses" when Mark called and asked for a woman whose name he didn't seem to know. Would he bother to keep up any sort of pretence? Or would he come straight out with it and announce that the woman staying there was in fact his wife?

I wondered if he would take Rhoda away from the inn, drive off in his car out of range of prying ears. To talk to Rhoda as Mark had to talk, they would need to be alone. Yet would he welcome the intimate atmosphere of a car, sitting there side by side?

In my tormented thoughts I found one small crumb of satisfaction. It was of no advantage to me, but vindictively I was glad to think of Rhoda's astonishment at Mark's arrival at the inn. She wouldn't have expected me to tell him about her call. To her distorted mind, it would be madness on my part. To Rhoda, handling a man was like playing a fish. I didn't know whether she really believed I would succumb to her blackmailing demands, but I was sure she would bank on me keeping my mouth shut.

With absolutely no appetite I made myself some breakfast. I had to do something. I was just sitting down to toast and coffee, wondering if I could possibly swallow a thing, when Mark burst in. He had been away hardly a quarter of an hour.

I jumped up, jarring the table, making the coffee cup rattle violently.

"What is it, Mark?"

"She wasn't there. Rhoda didn't stay at the 'Wagon and Horses' last night."

I gaped at him. "But she must have done. When she left me she was going straight to the pub."

"And so she did, apparently. She had another drink, and then cleared off again."

"But I thought she'd booked a room there. Where on earth could she have gone at that time of night?"

Mark frowned. "She might be anywhere. It's just like Rhoda to chop and change her mind like that. You never could rely on anything she said."

"Did they know who she was?" I asked.

"Oh no. It's pretty clear she wasn't recognized. But then, it's five years since . . . And anyway, she hardly ever came to the village when she was at Sherbridge."

"But what on earth did she tell them at the pub when she went out again?"

"Nothing," Mark said. "Except that she might or might not be wanting a room for the night. It all depended, she said."

"But what about her luggage?" I asked.

"Apparently she didn't have any with her."

I remembered the big shoulder bag. Rhoda could have carried enough in that for a night or two away.

"I suppose she must have realized there wasn't a hope of you changing your mind, so she decided to clear out." Mark sighed. "Where the devil has she gone? I've got to find her, I can't leave things the way they are. I imagine she must have been living in London somewhere—I can't see Rhoda going anywhere else once she got back to this country. On the other hand it looks as if she must have been staying in this locality for a while, to have found out about you . . ."

"She only heard about me . . . us . . . when she was at the pub earlier on. She boasted to me about how much information she'd picked up from the bar gossip. You see, she hadn't intended coming to me at first . . ."

"What low scheme had she in mind then? Did she tell you?"

I hated having to say it, but Mark was insistent.

"She meant to go and see your mother."

"Mother!" he exclaimed. "But why?"

"She said . . ." I swallowed nervously. "Rhoda said she believed Lady Galbraith would be willing to give her money—to avoid a scandal."

Mark put his hands up to his face, groaning. "Oh God! What a mess it all is." He looked up at me haggardly. "She's right—you know that? I really do believe Mother would submit to blackmail—*anything*, just so long as she preserved her wretched image of unblemished respectability. Heaven knows why, Jan, but she's always been like that. She just can't bear anything the least bit unsavoury to touch the family. I suppose it was stupid of me to pander to her—but I did. I never told her the reason why Rhoda and I were getting married in the first place. I suppose she must have guessed when we arranged it in such a rush, but the polite fiction was kept up that Rhoda and I were too much in love to wait, etcetera." He gave a harsh laugh. "It's pretty ridiculous when you think of it, feeling you've got to conceal the truth from your own mother. I never gave her the least clue that Rhoda and I didn't get on . . . That's why I played for time when Rhoda left me . . ."

I had been listening wide-eyed to all this. The picture Mark painted of his mother was not new to me. Even so, I was appalled to think that Lady Galbraith's own son thought her capable of paying a blackmailer. If not actually true, it was bad enough that her past behaviour allowed such an idea to cross his mind.

"You know Jan," Mark went on, "I've got a hunch that Rhoda did call on Mother last night. I was late getting home, I know, but Mother has always waited up for me before. It gets on my nerves sometimes the way she insists on doing what she thinks is her duty. And then this morning she still hadn't got up when I left. She called out to me that she had a headache and would lie in for a bit. But again, that's unlike Mother. She doesn't let such things as a headache get her down. No, something is behind her strange behaviour. I think Rhoda must have called on her and . . ."

"But Mark," I protested. "Just because your mother is upset, it's no reason to think . . . I mean, the mere fact of *seeing* Rhoda would have been enough. I'm sure she wouldn't have agreed to anything . . ."

"Maybe you're right, Jan. I hope so." Suddenly he made up his mind. "I'm going straight back home now to have it out with her. Will you come with me?"

"Me? But Mark, I'm sure your mother wouldn't want to see me. She won't want an outsider intruding."

"You're not an outsider, Jan, and Mother might just as well understand that. I want you to be there, so you can tell her what Rhoda said to you."

"But suppose, Mark, just suppose you're mistaken. If Rhoda wasn't at your house last night . . ."

He was shaking his head. "I know my mother, Jan. I was a fool not to realize before that something very odd was going on."

"But why should she conceal it from you? You would have to know in the end."

Mark was silent, looking at me with troubled eyes.

At length I said slowly, "You really do believe that your mother must have paid Rhoda to keep out of the way, don't you?"

"That's why I want you to come with me, Jan. I know it's a horrible thing to have to say, but unless I can confront Mother with the fact of Rhoda calling on you, I believe she might well try to deny the whole thing. I really do think it would help if you'd come too."

Reluctantly I agreed to go with him. I hated to push my way into what was such a private family matter, but after all, I was involved already.

Mark was looking around in a dazed fashion. "Where's the phone? I'll have to ring my office . . . I've got an appointment with an important client . . ."

His voice trailed off. His face was grey and he looked years older. I was filled with pity for him, pressed on all sides with worries. Even the strongest of men might break under such an intolerable strain. It wasn't as if it were his own business he was running. He couldn't leave it to take care of itself for the time being. Mark had accepted a trust from his uncle, and to abandon it now might have a disastrous effect on Lionel Buxton's health. So on top of all this personal agony, Mark was forced to think and plan for the factory too.

"Can't Derek . . . ?" I began.

"No, Derek can't!" This was the first and only time I heard Mark critical of his cousin.

It was still barely ten o'clock when Mark and I stood in the hall of his home. That elegant home, filled almost to choking point with austere regency-striped silence.

The voice that greeted us was unexpectedly jolly. Mrs. Bird came from the back of the house, wiping her hands on an apron.

"Why," she said surprised, "if it isn't Mr. Mark! What brings you back so soon?" Then she spotted me standing beside him, and went coy. "And you, Miss Janice. Well now, isn't that nice." She stood there looking at us with her perky sparrow's head on one side.

"Is my mother up yet, Mrs. Bird?" Mark asked seriously.

"Not yet, Mr. Mark. To tell you the truth, I've been a tiny bit worried about her. I took her up a cup of tea just now, and she looked ever so white and drawn. Like I told her, 'You ought to have the doctor in,' I said. I'm sure she's sickening for something . . ."

A frigid, chilling voice came from the head of the curving staircase. "Thank you, Mrs. Bird. That will be all."

These cold words sent the little woman scurrying off. You could almost see her flapping her wings in alarm. Mark and I, looking up, saw Lady Galbraith.

If I had expected to see any sign of agitation in Mark's mother, I was wrong. She stood there above us, a tall, commanding figure in a flawless pale green linen dress, her hair as perfectly in place as ever.

I felt certain that Mark had been mistaken in thinking that Rhoda had called on her.

"What is it, Mark?" she asked. "Why are you not at your office?" It was her voice that betrayed her. Behind the cultured, beautifully modulated tone there was an unease. Lady Galbraith was not as sure of herself as she wanted it to appear.

"I've got to talk to you, Mother," said Mark. "It's very important."

For the first time she allowed her gaze to take me in. "Janice Prior, too? This is early to be calling."

Mark took my arm. I wasn't sure whether it was to restrain me from speaking, or to demonstrate to his mother how useless it would be to try to come between us.

"Will you come down, please Mother." He spoke very firmly.

Lady Galbraith at first hesitated, then, as if detecting something ominous in her son's voice, she began to descend. She was still a majestic figure, but as she drew near I could see why she had chosen to remain in half shadow at the top of the stairs. Her face was ravaged, white and puffy. It was evident that she had suffered a severe shock.

Valiantly she tried to keep up the pretence. "Really Mark darling, couldn't it wait, whatever it is? I have so much to get through this morning. I have to be in Sherbridge by noon for a committee . . ."

"Come in here, Mother," Mark cut in. He opened the door to the drawing-room and waved her inside. He motioned me to follow her.

Lady Galbraith crossed the room and sat in a small boudoir chair beside the empty fireplace, her back straight, unsupported. I think she sat because she needed to, but she rested her hands upon her lap with apparent calm.

"Now Mark," she said. "What is all this nonsense about?"

Mark frowned. "I want you to tell me what occurred last night!"

She tried to bluff it out. "What occurred? What on earth do you mean? I spent the evening alone, as you well know. And I went to bed with a headache."

"No, you were not alone, Mother. You had a visitor, didn't you?" I saw that he was giving her the chance to be the first to mention Rhoda's name.

"Really, Mark! As I told you . . ."

He was impatient. "Mother! Please tell me the truth. I happen to know—because she went to see Jan, too."

Her eyes hardened. She glared at me as if it were an impertinence to intrude upon her life in this way. "She went to see *you?*" Her voice rose sharply in pitch. "But why? Why should she?"

There was no satisfaction in Mark's voice. He spoke flatly. "So you admit Rhoda *did* come to see you?"

For a moment I thought Lady Galbraith was going to persist in her lying. It looked as if she would defy her son to drag the truth out of her. But then the hands in her lap parted in a little gesture of helplessness. In that instant I warmed slightly to Lady Galbraith. I felt sorry for her.

"Yes," she admitted in defeat. "She did come here. When I saw who it was, I nearly fainted."

"You should have told me, Mother. Why on earth did you try to hide it?"

Lady Galbraith rallied, looking up at him proudly. "I wanted to spare you, Mark. That woman was never any good to you."

"Mother, you are not to treat me like a child. Now then, what happened between you and Rhoda?"

I could sense that it was the first time Mark had spoken to his mother like this. Perhaps he was to blame for letting her give the impression that she was still mothering him. He had too readily allowed her to have her own way. She was a woman who needed opposition.

At all events, Lady Galbraith made no attempt to fight back at Mark. Instead, she turned on me.

"Rhoda did not tell me she had been to see you last night. I suppose that is the reason you telephoned. Why did you not tell me then that you had seen her?"

"I . . . I didn't want to worry you, Lady Galbraith."

"But you had no right . . ." She became slightly hysterical. "*Anything* that concerns Mark is my business."

Mark interrupted, but he was more gentle now. "Jan was absolutely right not to tell you about Rhoda until she'd spoken to me."

"But if I'd known, I wouldn't have . . ." She stopped abruptly, as if sensing danger ahead.

"What wouldn't you have done, Mother?"

"It doesn't matter." She closed her lips firmly.

"It does matter, Mother. It matters very

much." Getting no response to this he went on grimly, "Rhoda tried to blackmail Jan last night."

Lady Galbraith was startled, there was no doubt about that. But it was also very apparent that she was annoyed. Again there was a suggestion in the air that it was sheer insolence on my part to be involved in this matter.

"Why should Rhoda have attempted to do that?" she asked coldly.

This time Mark didn't hold back to spare her feelings. "Because she knew that Jan and I love one another."

I saw his mother flinch.

Mark went on, "*Of course* Jan refused to have any truck with her. But something she said made us realize she might well have come to see you. She was supposed to be staying at the 'Wagon and Horses' last night, but she didn't."

Lady Galbraith was triumphant. "No, she left the village—and she will not be returning."

"What do you mean? I've got to find her, surely you understand that?"

"Let her be, Mark! Don't you see, you

are well rid of her. She won't be bothering you again—you can take my word for it."

Mark's black suspicions were being justified. He maintained a surface calm, but I could see what an effort it cost him to restrain his anger. I stood watching the battle between these two, mother and son, not daring to intervene in the slightest way.

"Mother, tell me at once everything that happened between you. And I want the truth."

Perhaps it was seeing something of herself coming out in Mark that made Lady Galbraith tremble. Not pride, but determined refusal to be deflected. Their eyes met in silent conflict, and then at last she looked away, beaten. He had proved the stronger.

She said quietly, her words barely audible, "I gave her money . . . Twenty pounds."

"Mother!" The sharp voice was a warning. "Rhoda would not have settled for a mere twenty pounds. She'd want a lot more than that. Either you know where she is, so you can send the money on, or she's coming back for it. Which way is it?"

"I told you, she won't be coming back. I . . . I gave her a cheque."

"She wouldn't have accepted a cheque —it could so easily be stopped."

His mother shook her head. "She said I wouldn't dare to. She threatened to make trouble if I stopped payment." Now Lady Galbraith seemed oblivious of me. She turned imploring eyes on Mark. "Let her go, darling. Nobody else need know . . ."

"Mother! Don't be ridiculous. *Of course* I've got to find her."

"But everyone else in the world believes that your wife died in that fire. Why not leave it at that? Why rake up what is past and done with?"

Mark spoke with great restraint, as if to a small child who could not understand. "I know now that Rhoda is alive. I cannot turn my back on that knowledge."

"But my boy, can't you see? If you find her, people will know. We shall never be able to keep it secret."

"Naturally people will know. What does that matter?"

Only now was I to realize just *how* desperate Lady Galbraith had become. She tried a new tactic which must have cost her a great deal. She was prepared to go to any lengths to avoid a scandalous exposure.

"Mark, please! You tell me that you and Janice love one another. This way, with that woman gone, you will be able to get married."

She broke down, pleading with Mark, begging him to do as she asked. It was pitiful to see this regal figure reduced to grovelling. Mark tried to stop her, but she went on and on, tears streaming down her face.

I could almost find it in my heart to accept her suggestion. Loving as we did, couldn't Mark and I take one another on almost any terms? If we could be sure that Rhoda would stay away . . .

It was a devil's dream of happiness, a mirage of contentment, just as this elegant room was false evidence of tranquil and dignified living. Nothing would be real in our lives. No joy, no permanence.

Angrily, Mark stormed at his mother, demanding to know where Rhoda was. But in the end he had to accept the plain fact that Lady Galbraith could give him no help.

"She's gone, I say—gone. I don't know where. And I thank God I cannot tell you."

She was so distraught by this time that Mark decided his mother had better go back to bed. Amazingly, she made no protest, even when he asked me to help her.

We made our way slowly up to her room. I had never seen it before. Even more than the rest of this immaculate house, it was so utterly perfect in every detail that it was hardly real. All except the bed. Still unmade, it bore signs of a restless sleeper.

In the extremity of her grief, Lady Galbraith still cared about me seeing the rumpled bed.

"That slipshod Mrs. Bird," she said petulantly. "It should have been made by now."

This was nonsense, of course. The bed had hardly been vacated—it was still warm. I straightened it without comment.

Lady Galbraith disappeared into what I imagined was her dressing-room, and emerged a few minutes later in a gold silk

146

negligee. She had managed to regain some of her usual poise.

"Thank you, Janice. It is kind of you," she said with dignity, but the old hauteur had gone. I supposed she realized I'd heard too much that morning to be treated as a complete outsider.

"Shall I ask Mrs. Bird to make you some coffee?" I said. "Would you like that, Lady Galbraith?"

"Thank you, no. I shall be better resting."

I went to the door, but suddenly the slender shred of pride dissolved. She was in tears again.

"Janice . . . my dear. Make him see. Mark loves you—he would listen to you."

Only a fanatical craving for respectability—respectability at all costs, would have brought Lady Galbraith to such straits. How otherwise could she have demeaned herself by entreating me to use my influence with Mark? How could she admit that another woman, any other woman, might possibly be able to sway her son where she herself was impotent?

She was sitting up in bed, a hand held out to me, imploring. I had to feel sorry for her. One can only feel pity at seeing another human being reduced to such weakness.

I tried to smile at her as I left the room, but I felt there was nothing else I could do.

Mrs. Bird was in the hall, busy with a mop on the speckless banister rails. She knew something dramatic was afoot, and she wasn't going to miss anything, not if she could help it.

I gave her a half-smile as I passed—a non-committal smile. Then I went into the drawing-room and carefully shut the door behind me.

Mark swung round to face me.

"Jan darling, I mustn't involve you in this sordid mess any more."

"I'm in it now, Mark," I said quietly. "And I am going to give you any help I can." I wouldn't have wanted it any other way. Mark's troubles were my troubles, and I couldn't visualize turning my back on him now.

He reached out and gripped my hand. "You're so good to me, Jan." The weight of his problems took over again, and he paced away. "If only we had a clue, some sort of lead. Rhoda could be anywhere by now."

"But Mark, surely she must still be in the district. She's got to cash your mother's cheque. If we wait around at the bank, she's bound to turn up. Rhoda won't leave it long—she'll want to get away from here."

He shook his head. "Mother banks in London—at the City Guilds."

I might have guessed. Not for Lady Galbraith were the banks of the common run. The City Guilds was a classy merchant banking house. There would be a certain cachet about having an account with them.

Mark looked at me suddenly. "I've a good mind to get on to the police and have them catch her when she presents that wretched cheque. But how can I? I can't let Mother be dragged in. I don't know whether conniving at blackmail is a criminal charge, but in any case the publicity alone would break her. She'd never be able to stand the . . . disgrace— that's how she'd think of it."

I had an idea.

"Mark, I've just thought. If you tell the

bank to stop payment of that cheque, Rhoda would be furious about it, and she'd get after your mother right away. She'd either write or else come down here again herself. Either way, we'll be on to her."

Mark's eyes brightened. "Jan, I think you've got it."

"That is," I warned him cautiously, "unless Rhoda's been to the bank already."

We turned together to look at the clock.

"Eleven-fifteen," he said gloomily. "She won't hang on long to a cheque like that." He picked up the phone. "We'll just have to hope . . ."

8

SUDDENLY I felt exhausted and sat down. Mark had been put through to an official at the bank.

"Could you please tell me if a cheque on my mother's account has been presented yet?" He gave the details. "Yes, it would have been this morning, if at all."

He stood there, bent over the phone, impatiently drumming his long fingers on the table. Then I saw a look of relief cross his face.

"Good! My mother will be confirming this in writing, of course, but meantime will you please accept my authority to stop payment? Thank you. Oh, by the way, could you arrange for someone to telephone me at my office immediately the cheque is presented?" He gave the number. "It's very important that we should know."

From the time Mark put down the phone we were expecting a call from the bank every minute. A day passed without news, a second, a third. We felt helpless until we knew Rhoda had been to the bank. Then we could expect her to contact Lady Galbraith. Mark and I would have to keep watch for her, somehow, because we knew without putting it into words that Lady Galbraith could not be trusted. She might well send Rhoda away again, with a new cheque, saying nothing to Mark.

The factory continued to demand Mark's full attention. The strain was beginning to show, but even so I think he was better for having other worries. It meant that at least for brief periods he could forget . . .

Forgetting was something I couldn't do. I lived and ate and slept with our problem, often waking up in the night with a feeling of terror. Once I was awake, the fright would subside, and a numb despair possessed me. I would lie there restlessly tossing in the bed, until I was driven to creep downstairs and make myself tea— just to give my hands something to do. Afterwards I would wash up the one cup and put things back into place, not wanting Aunt Frank to comment. It was unlikely she'd notice anything unusual, even when it was under her nose. But I couldn't risk exposing myself to her solicitude. I should never be able to keep silent.

So for three days I had to try to keep up an appearance of normality. The only thing Aunt Frank commented on was my refusal of food. She herself always had a hearty appetite. "You must eat, my dear, to keep up your strength."

Mrs. Buxton was far more perceptive. I would see her looking at me curiously, and I knew she had none of Aunt Frank's inhibitions about prying. Whenever I was alone with her for more than a minute or two, I was obliged to take evasive action, finding an excuse to go back to Mr. Buxton, or even seeking out Derek quite deliberately.

Not so long ago I would have found it difficult to shake Derek off. But now it did begin to look as if my persistent refusals were having some effect. Instead of pressing me all the time to go out with him again, he would sit around in a morose silence, watching me, and having one or two drinks too many.

He walked back to Mead Cottage with me one night, looking very flushed and sulky. I tried to make innocuous conversation by talking about his uncle and aunt, but got no response.

At last, in a quiet spot near the old stone bridge, he stopped and faced me, gripping my arm hard above the elbow.

"We can't go on like this, Jan," he said hoarsely.

I dreaded a scene with Derek. In a tiny village the news would soon get around, and it would make life even more unpleasant. I particularly wanted to avoid the Buxtons' hearing that we had quarrelled.

"Derek," I said, trying to be calm and objective. "Don't say anything you might be sorry about later."

"Sorry be damned!" he cried. "I'll never be sorry for saying how I feel about you."

I shook my head. "But it's no good, Derek. I've told you so already . . ."

"Can't you get over this . . . *fixation* about Mark?" he burst out. "With you it's nothing but Mark all the time. A cold fish like him!"

The idea of Mark being cold was ludicrous, but I wouldn't let Derek bait me into arguing about it. "I must get home," I said.

Derek wouldn't give up. I had noticed him put down three or four whiskies that evening, and I suppose they were having an effect. He gripped my shoulders so tightly that it hurt.

"Come out with a real man for once," he urged, rather thickly. "You just don't know what you're missing."

When I jerked away from him he was contrite. "No, I didn't mean it that way, Jan darling. Please . . . please listen."

But I was already walking on. Even if it did provoke an open quarrel, I'd had enough of Derek for the moment. He ran after me, pleading with me to forgive him. "I've said I'm sorry, Jan. Give me a chance to put it right. Come out with me one evening—you enjoyed it that time at the 'Chequers'."

We had reached the cottage by now. I went straight in the gate, shutting it firmly behind me.

"Thank you for bringing me home, Derek," I said coldly. I walked in and closed the door while he was still protesting.

On the fourth day of our unhappy vigil, that period of limbo while Mark and I awaited a move from Rhoda, I was washing-up the lunch things with Aunt Frank. In theory, I was helping her, but in practice she was holding a teacloth and gazing out of the window into the blue distance. She pondered a knotty problem of crossword juxtaposition, her lips moving slightly in the abstracted way she had.

The phone rang in the sitting-room. Aunt Frank didn't even hear it, and I'm pretty sure she didn't notice that I dashed off to answer it.

It was Mark, and at last he seemed to have some news. But he wouldn't tell me anything on the phone.

"I've got to talk to you, Jan. I don't want to call at Mead Cottage just now, so I'll wait for you by the bridge. Can you be there in five minutes?"

Mark's voice was enough to warn me that something was seriously wrong. When I met him, his face confirmed my fears.

He was pacing up and down by the car, impatiently waiting for me.

As I drew near, a woman walked past him, and I heard her say, "Good afternoon, Mr. Galbraith."

She had to speak again before he answered. It was so unlike Mark. He was usually so carefully and charmingly polite.

He opened the car door for me. "Jump in," he said briefly. And at once we were driving through the village street and climbing the hill past the Buxtons' house. I didn't ask what was the matter—this was not the place for an explanation. We sat together in silence until we were over the brow of the hill, and he had drawn into a small lane leading to the disused stone quarries. It was quiet here—nobody was in sight.

Mark pulled on the handbrake slowly, carefully, then switched off the engine. He made these simple movements elaborately, as though glad of the opportunity they afforded for delay.

At last he turned to me. He spoke in a flat, emotionless voice, as if he knew of no other way of breaking such news.

"Rhoda's body has been found washed

up a few miles along the coast, towards Weymouth."

"*Oh, Mark!*"

"She had been murdered. There's no doubt about it, Jan. She was strangled, and then presumably her body was dumped into the sea."

I gasped with horror, yet in a way I think I was half prepared for some such awful news. The delay in presenting Lady Galbraith's cheque had made me fear that something dreadful had happened, though I had never allowed my mind to be specific.

"When . . . when do they think she was killed?"

"They're saying it was about four days ago."

We could not meet one another's eyes. We both knew what this meant. Soon after coming to see me, probably within hours, Rhoda had been brutally killed. I had a sudden picture of her, vital and alive, mocking me, careless of the effect of her actions upon others. I remembered how incredibly beautiful she had looked, even with hair straggling wet with the rain.

"How did you hear about this?" I asked Mark.

"The police came round . . ."

My eyes widened. "They knew she was your wife?"

"No, there was nothing to show who she was."

"It was the cheque, then—your mother's cheque?"

But Mark shook his head wearily. "No, the cheque wasn't found. It was pure chance that brought the police to me. They soon circulated a description of her, and the local constable here in the village, old Bob Frinton, remembered Rhoda coming to *Elgin House* that night. At least, he saw her standing by the front door, waiting to be let in. Of course, in a tiny place like this, the policeman notices a strange face."

"So they came to ask you who she was?"

"Maybe that's all they had in mind at the time. I wasn't in when they called, and unfortunately they talked to Mother. She was alarmed at being questioned, and denied any knowledge of Rhoda. She said nobody had been to the house that evening. So then Sergeant Hayes came to see me at the office. I've known him for years, and he was friendly enough. But he made it pretty plain that he knew Mother was concealing something. He showed me a picture of Rhoda and I had to admit who she was. I didn't tell him *all* the truth—I wanted to avoid getting Mother into trouble—so I merely said it looked like my wife who I hadn't seen for a year, and who I had believed was dead." He paused and ran a finger round inside his collar, as though he felt stifled by it. "They asked me to go and identify the body."

"Oh Mark!" I reached out and took his hand. It was deadly cold.

"After that the police drove me home and interviewed Mother and me together. It all had to come out. I was a fool not to see that before."

"What did the police say when they discovered that neither of you had really told them the truth?"

"The sergeant took a pretty dim view of it, I can tell you. But he was very decent. I think he was embarrassed at having to question us, because it was obvious that something unsavoury was being unearthed. In the end I told him everything—except that Rhoda had been to see you first."

"But you should have told them that, too, Mark. It will only make things more difficult for you when they find out."

"There's no reason why they *should* find out—Mother said nothing. I want to keep you out of this, Jan. You've had quite enough of my family troubles—more than enough."

"But I want to help you, Mark. I don't mind the police knowing."

He smiled his gratitude, and touched my arm. "You've already helped more than you can understand just by being here, darling." His face clouded again. He looked down at the steering wheel and began to fiddle with the gear lever. "Actually, I really don't think it would help in the least if it came out about Rhoda calling on you. It might even . . . complicate things."

I was bewildered. Then the significance of his words sank in, and I shivered. The police were perhaps already thinking that Mark could well be involved in Rhoda's death. It was, after all, a ghastly coincidence that she should have been killed so

161

soon after her reappearance here. The village gossip, which Rhoda had picked up so easily, would not have escaped the police. If they knew that Rhoda had called at Mead Cottage and threatened me, just as she had threatened Lady Galbraith, they would consider there was a powerful case against Mark.

Something niggled at the back of my mind.

"Mark, did they find Rhoda's handbag with the body?"

"Yes, apparently they did."

"Then why wasn't your mother's cheque in it? Either there or in a pocket?"

Mark's lips tightened. "All I know is that they didn't find it—or the twenty pounds."

Could Lady Galbraith have been lying about giving Rhoda money and a cheque? I tried to push the thought out of my mind, but it refused to go. I remembered now that it was only when Mark insisted he knew Rhoda had been to see her, that his mother had spoken of a cheque. But was it really likely that a blackmailer would risk accepting something that could be traced back? I doubted it. I remembered too how upset Lady Galbraith had become when Mark told her that he was determined to find Rhoda. Almost hysterically she had cried, "She's gone, I tell you —gone."

Lady Galbraith would know as well as anyone else that a blackmailer always comes back for more. She could have had no faith in any promise Rhoda made to her. Perhaps she had found a better way of silencing Rhoda! Perhaps she had made certain that Mark's wife would never return again to cause a scandal!

"It wasn't necessarily anyone from around here who killed her," I said. "Somebody may have followed her."

It was more to still my own suspicions than because I thought it likely.

The way Mark seized upon the suggestion was enough to tell me his thoughts had been following the same horrible direction as my own. Poor Mark! It was a dreadful thing for *me* to imagine that Lady Galbraith could be responsible for Rhoda's death. How much worse it must be for him to think that about his own mother!

He turned my half-hearted suggestion to

firm fact. "Yes, Jan, that's it," he cried. "I'm sure you're right."

"Of course," I said uneasily, "whoever it was must have had cause to hate her."

"Rhoda was the sort to leave a trail of enemies," Mark said, enlarging the crack of hope I had opened for him. "When you think of the way she carried on—caring for no one but herself. Any number of people must have hated her."

Then I remembered something else—something Rhoda herself had told me. It wasn't much, but it helped lend substance to our tenuous theory. The theory we were constructing against the evidence the police would think so clear cut.

"Mark, she was living with some man until quite recently. No, I don't mean the one she . . . she ran off with. Rhoda told me she left *him* months ago, and found someone else. She actually boasted to me how she'd helped this man get through his money and had then thrown him over. Surely *he* would have had a motive?"

"Of course! Did she say who he was—where they were living?"

"No," I said, feeling miserably inadequate. "She didn't even mention his name."

"Still," said Mark, grimly holding on to hope. "No doubt the police will find him. I . . . I'll try to think of a way of telling Sergeant Hayes about him without admitting how I know."

And that's how we had to leave it. We sat there talking for a long time. The warm June sun mocked us with its joyful brilliance as we tried to see our way through this fearful situation. But the end seemed dark—how dark we dared not confess to one another.

9

THE details of Rhoda's death would be all over Bishop's Cranford in next to no time. In an isolated rural community sensational news flashed around with the speed of light.

Everybody in the village knew about Mark and me—everybody, that is, except the one whose hospitality I was enjoying. Aunt Frank, I felt sure, was happily oblivious of our love affair. But I couldn't in decency let her remain in ignorance. It just wouldn't be fair to allow her to learn about Mark and me from a malicious tongue. Before, it wouldn't have mattered. I doubt in fact if Aunt Frank would have taken it in. But now with a murder attached to the story, it would be forced upon even her wayward attention.

I resolved to tell her right away, as soon as I got home.

Aunt Frank was having an afternoon cup of tea. When I came in she was standing by the sink in the kitchen, looking into space. She waved vaguely at the teapot on the draining board. I hated interrupting her in a creative mood, but this time I had to.

"Aunt Frank," I said in a firm voice. "I want to talk to you. It's very important."

At once, without resentment, she gave me her full attention. I thanked heaven for her calm detachment as she listened to my story. There was no fussing, no waste of breath in exclamation and bewailment. She heard me out sympathetically, cutting in once or twice when a point needed clarification.

All this time we had been standing in the kitchen. When I had finished at last, she took my arm and led me into the sitting-room.

She sat me down on the settle and herself beside me, still holding my arm.

"My poor child, what a lot of trouble you've been through—and all without a word to me. Now you must promise you'll never let that happen again. I'm here to help, you know. I like to think you would come to me as readily as you would to your own mother."

She didn't realize how much *more*

readily I could confide in her! If it was Mother I was talking to now, my easily flustered mother, all the strength would have to come from me.

But not Aunt Frank.

"Of course," she was saying, "I knew you were fond of Mark, and that you and he have been going out quite a lot together. But I admit I didn't appreciate the true situation. I must say I think you would be very well suited—he is a very pleasant young man, clever and most considerate."

Oddly enough I came nowhere near to crying. I looked at Aunt Frank, dry eyed, and spoke heavily. "Well, all hope of that is gone now."

"Why should you think so?" Her tone was a reprimand.

I avoided the question. "If only I could help Mark," I cried. "Things look so black for him. I know I ought to tell the police that Rhoda came here that night, but he made me promise I wouldn't."

Aunt Frank digested this. Nothing she said was ever unconsidered. "I'm sure you'll find that before long you will be obliged to tell them. It's a mistake to think that anything can be hushed up in such an investigation."

I nodded miserably. "I'll speak to Mark again. Perhaps he will agree."

It was a relief to talk to someone as clear thinking as my aunt. "You must have faith in the police," she said. "They'll get at the truth of the matter. It's a question of sifting every grain of information they can gather—that's why I say you shouldn't try to conceal anything from them. It's in your own interest to be quite open."

The next twenty-four hours were black for me, but compared with what was to follow it was almost a happy period. Mark telephoned to tell me that the police had called again at his office. Sergeant Hayes wanted some proof of what Mark had been doing on the evening Rhoda was believed to have been killed.

"I haven't got an alibi," Mark told me in a crushed sort of voice. "I was working here until ten-thirty, and you know what Sherbridge is like after dark. The whole place is dead."

Although it was well known that Mark often stayed late at the factory, apparently there wasn't a soul who could or would testify to his being there on that particular night. Nobody saw him come out, nobody could be found who so much as saw the light shining from his uncurtained office.

"If only I'd dropped in at the café for a sandwich," he said. "I do sometimes. I didn't need to get any petrol, either. I had no contact with a single other person that night, from the time the factory staff left. I didn't even see Mother when I got home."

There was a short silence. Mention of Lady Galbraith seemed to give us both a shock. Again we avoided saying what was in our minds.

"It gets you down," he said, "the way the police ask question after question. I suppose it's only a routine enquiry, really. The husband is always the first suspect, I believe."

"Mark!" I cried out in anguish. "How can they even think it was you?"

"You can't blame them. We've got to admit it looks pretty black. I know I'm being kept under observation already—I can recognize most of the police chaps in Sherbridge."

"You mean you're being *followed?*"

"Well, they're keeping a close eye on

me. But I think it will go further than that any time now."

"You mean you think they'll . . . ?"

His voice seemed harsh, bitter, not like Mark. "Helping the police with their enquiries—I think that's the phrase."

"But they must be making lots of other enquiries. What about Rhoda's life in London? What about that man . . . ?"

"They didn't seem to be interested in the possibility of her being involved with other men. In fact, I got the impression they thought it was just a red herring I'd dragged in. It's perfectly obvious that I'm their chief suspect—or rather, their only suspect."

It was frightening to feel so helpless when Mark was in such danger. But what could I do? However much I fought against it, the idea wheedled its insidious way into my brain. Mark could only clear himself by laying suspicion on his mother. Her coldly aristocratic figure loomed over all other thoughts, and would not be banished.

Long after midnight I was still threshing about in bed, sleepless with fear and worry. I myself began to clutch at the same straw I had offered Mark. The murderer might not be a local person after all. During the early hours of the morning the idea grew in my mind until it assumed a real possibility, even a probability.

On the face of it, perhaps it might appear unlikely that Rhoda should be killed here in Dorset by somebody she had known in London. But was it such a wild theory? A man with a bitter grudge against her might have been on her trail for some time, waiting for an opportunity. And in this quiet rural spot his chance would have come.

I couldn't understand why the police had seemed so uninterested in Rhoda's activities before she came to Bishop's Cranford. Mark hadn't dared to admit that he actually knew she had been living with another man—this would have meant disclosing *how* he knew, and mentioning my name. But it must have been obvious to the police that a woman like Rhoda would certainly have been involved with some man or other.

I knew not only that there *had* been a man, but that Rhoda had deserted him shamefully. From my knowledge of her, I could well imagine how she would have taunted him with his uselessness now that the money had run out, scornfully telling him that she was on to something better. Wasn't that motive enough? He could have been on her trail ever since . . .

As the long night hours dragged by, I became more and more certain that this man must be Rhoda's killer. But if the police were so unwilling to enquire into Rhoda's past to look for an unknown man, what could we do about it?

There must be some way in which I could help Mark. To rescue him from the cloud of suspicion that threatened to engulf him.

Feverishly, I dissected my conversation with Rhoda. As accurately as I could recall it, I reconstructed every word she uttered, sifting for the smallest clue. It seemed to lead me nowhere. What did I know about this latest lover of hers? Just one tiny thing; that he had come into a few hundred pounds which she had helped him to spend. Whether the money came from betting, or a legacy, or from some criminal activity, I had no idea.

He hadn't been able to keep her in the

style she expected. What was it she'd told me? "A scruffy little dump"—those were her words. There was something else, though, and it bothered me. A casual remark she had thrown out just wouldn't come back to my mind. I worried at it ceaselessly, lying there in a sweat. But only when I gave up at last and tried to sleep, did the answer pop into my unprepared mind.

A scruffy little dump in the Barrows.

Couldn't I trace it from that? Surely the Barrows was an unusual name? I was excited at the idea and sat up in bed, pulling blankets round me.

Mark had been so sure that Rhoda would live nowhere but London, if she could help it. There couldn't be many places with that name there. And if the Barrows could be pinned down, surely the man she had been living with could be traced?

Suddenly I knew what I must do. I must go to London myself and try to locate this man. If the police wouldn't bother, then it was up to me. I would get their evidence for them, and hand it over on a plate.

It was twenty-past-six by now. I got up

and dressed quietly. Mark would stop me if he knew, and I was afraid Aunt Frank might also be against such a trip. I had a small case with me, and packed it with things to carry me over a night or two. Then I crept downstairs and hastily swallowed a glass of milk.

The railway timetable was a disappointment. There was a fast train to London at seven-thirty, and nothing more until ten o'clock. This one anyhow was horribly slow, stopping at nearly every station on the way. I knew there was no bus out of the village until eight o'clock, by which time Aunt Frank would be moving.

I looked at my watch again. Ten-to-seven! There was just time, if I could beg a lift.

Hastily rinsing the glass, I scribbled a note to say I'd had an idea which might possibly be helpful, and that I'd gone to London. I asked Aunt Frank to tell Mark when he phoned. By then I'd be well on the way.

There wasn't a soul about when I went out. The morning sun, shining at an unfamilar angle, sparked off the buildings, throwing deep shadows. I hurried along, not wanting to be seen, to be questioned.

Three hundred yards past the end of the village I came to the main road, where I could expect to meet occasional traffic. Within two minutes a rather sedate car came along, driven by an elderly and respectable looking man. I signalled frantically, giving the hitch-hikers' sign with my thumb.

He stopped at once and leaned across to the window.

"Where do you want to go?" he asked with a smile, touching his hat.

"Sherbridge, please."

"Hop in. I'm going right through there."

As we drove off I explained about wanting to get the early train. "I couldn't get a bus, you see, and the garage isn't open yet for a taxi."

"That's all right," he said. "Glad to have some company."

He told me he was going to an agricultural conference at Exeter, and had already been on the road an hour. He was a gossipy old man, but I had to humour him because he was kind enough to give me a lift.

"Wasn't that Bishop's Cranford you came from?" he asked.

"That's right."

"Lot of excitement you've had there these last few days. I read all about that murder. Terrible business, wasn't it?"

A shudder ran through me. I could feel beads of perspiration breaking out on my forehead. In a controlled voice I told him I was a visitor to the village and really knew very little about the murder.

I had hoped to prevent any further discussion of Rhoda's death, but he took my words as an invitation to give me a detailed and lengthy account of all he had heard and read about it. I caught a note of morbid thrill in his voice.

"It's sure to have been the husband," he finished up.

The inevitability of his attitude chilled me.

"Why should you think that?" I asked carefully. "I expect there were other men in her life—she sounds that sort of woman. It could be one of them."

He laughed good-humouredly, but in

contempt. "Not a chance! You mark my words, it was that husband of hers all right. He had reason enough, after all."

"Reason enough?" I echoed, ice cold.

"Well, they're saying he had a girl friend he wanted to marry. So he had to make sure the first wife was well and truly dead this time."

I wanted to scream out at him for condemning Mark so blindly. I had to remind myself it was no more than most people would think, even if they didn't voice their opinions so openly. I trembled, imagining the talk in the "Wagon and Horses"—especially in the public bar, where women were never seen, and the conversation would be crudely masculine . . .

I was thankful when we reached the station. I just couldn't have taken any more of such unfair judgement.

But there was no escape for me. In the refreshment room, when I went to get myself a cup of coffee, the woman behind the counter, a porter, and a fat man with a newspaper, were busily discussing the murder.

The fat man was wagging a finger at his

paper. "It says here that the police expect to be in a position to make an arrest soon."

"That don't prove nothing," the porter scoffed. "They always say that. They got to kid the public along a bit. Besides, they hope it'll make the murderer give hisself away."

The woman pushed across my coffee without so much as glancing at me. She was far too absorbed in the conversation.

"Still," she said, "I shouldn't think it will take them long. It's pretty obvious, isn't it? What a shock he must have had —her turning up like that, and him thinking she'd been dead all this time."

The fat man guffawed. "Ha ha, *very* awkward!"

Leaving my coffee untasted I turned and ran. I couldn't bear it. I hadn't realized how protected I had been from idle gossip in Bishop's Cranford itself. Knowing who I was, the people in the village must have avoided any talk of the murder in my hearing. I had, though, been only too conscious of interested glances from everyone I met—glances that were both curious and in the main sympathetic.

It was not until I was settled in the

train, racing through the Dorset countryside, that my violent anger began to subside, lulled by the rhythmic, soothing hammering of the wheels.

So far this morning I'd been intent only on getting away from Bishop's Cranford undetected. I'd hardly given a thought to my plan of action.

Now I channelled my concentration on the task ahead. It wasn't going to be easy. I pictured myself discovering the Barrows, only to find nobody who knew Rhoda. How could I describe her, and how explain my interest? No pictures of Rhoda had appeared in the papers.

My mission was to trace a murderer. Already I was convinced of that. I didn't bother to work out what to do when I had unearthed him. Time enough when I got close.

I could tell people in the locality that I was looking for a girl of about twenty-four, petite, with black hair and brown eyes. As I tried to visualize her face I remembered Mrs. Buxton saying that Rhoda was in some ways very like me. Her suggestion that Mark had been drawn to marry her because of this resemblance, I had found strangely comforting at the time.

An idea crossed my mind, and impetuously, I had to act right away. I fumbled along the swaying corridor, and locked myself in the lavatory. Slipping off my nylon headband, I combed my hair forward, allowing it to fall half across my face just as I had seen Rhoda's that night. Then I began to notice the likeness for myself. With heavier make-up, I might easily pass for her sister.

The scheme had a double advantage. If I claimed to be Rhoda's sister, and spun a tale about having lost touch with her over the years, it would explain the reason for my enquiries. At the same time I could say she was rather like me, which might well help to jog somebody's memory.

I went back to my compartment with a hope that grew as each mile passed. It looked as if my far-fetched plan had some small chance of succeeding.

When we reached Paddington, I made straight for the nearest Post Office. I was in luck. The directory confirmed that there *was* only one Barrows in London—in the neighbourhood of Bloomsbury. My search was confined to one limited area. It might be difficult to find any trace of Rhoda, but at least I knew I would be searching in the right place.

I took a taxi to one of the Oxford Street stores and bought make-up. Scarlet lipstick like Rhoda had used, eye shadow, false lashes. Then I retired to the powder room.

Working on my face and hair I watched with a sort of horrible fascination as my own personality gradually disappeared, and another one took over. I didn't like what I saw. Rhoda had sufficient beauty to conceal her essential cheapness and vulgarity. Applied to me these qualities became apparent.

I realized that the powder room attendant was watching me with some surprise. In the mirror I caught her glance.

"You don't want to overdo it, love," she said. "You looked pretty enough the way you were."

"It's . . . it's my boy friend," I said hastily. "He wanted me to brighten myself up a bit."

She shook her head. "There's no pleasing men!" she exclaimed. "But if I had a nice complexion like yours, there's no man living I'd change it for, I can tell you."

There was another thing I had to do. Thankful that I had remembered to bring my cheque book, I went down to the rainwear department. I found a whole rack of raincoats like the one Rhoda had worn, and sorted out my size. There was no earthly reason why Rhoda's long lost sister should choose a similar type of coat, but they were common enough. I worked on the theory that it was one more aid to help jog someone's memory into recognition.

In the taxi, on my way to the Barrows, I developed this theory still further. I began to practise one or two little tricks and mannerisms of Rhoda's I had noticed. It struck me that such things stand more chance of awakening a vague memory than a superficial likeness. I took out my handbag mirror and tried flickering my eyelashes. This provocative habit must have been such a part of Rhoda's personality that she couldn't help doing it, even when there was no man around to captivate. Then I remembered a little gesture she had made several times—a sort of throw-away movement of her hand as she talked, and I practised that too.

Suddenly, I was aware of the coat I had changed from. I was carrying it on my arm. I got the driver to stop for a minute near Euston Square station while I disposed of my coat and small case in the left luggage office there.

I was all set to play the part of Rhoda's sister.

10

THE taxi pulled up in a leafy square of late-Georgian terraced houses. Still charming in their way, but sadly run down now from their original state.

"Well," said the driver, twisting round. "This is the Barrows. Where exactly did you want, Miss?"

I glanced up at the tall, grimy buildings, uncertain. "I don't know," I admitted. "You'd better drop me here, and I'll look around."

The driver shook his head doubtfully. "It's not just this square, you know. What they call the Barrows is all the streets leading out of it, too."

Feeling forlorn, I stood there on the pavement, gazing around at the dozens of houses, each one obviously divided into several flats and furnished rooms. And the driver said this was only a part of it! I began to feel thoroughly cast down.

Round the corner I stumbled into one

of those little clusters of small shops that can suddenly give London an intimate atmosphere. Very cosmopolitan little delicatessen and fancy continental bakers were cheek-by-jowl with the dowdiest of English drapers. How I would have enjoyed it in other circumstances!

I decided to make a start in the grocers shops, arguing that everybody must eat. The first one I came to was small, with only one assistant. I hung around in the background until the proprietor himself had finished serving. Then I moved forward, and spoke tentatively.

"I wonder if you could help me?" I began.

He looked at me warily. Something in my manner obviously told him I wasn't going to buy anything.

"I . . . I know this must sound odd, but I'm trying to trace my sister, and I wondered if by chance you could help me."

Fortunately, there were no customers in the shop now. The young assistant casually moved nearer, and I could sense that he had pricked up his ears. He pretended to be neatening a stack of tinned peas.

The grocer looked puzzled. He must have thought I was as stupid as I felt. "What's her name, then?"

"That's the trouble, I don't know." Seeing the look in his eye, I hastened on with my prepared explanation. "You see, she's married now and I don't know her new name. I . . . I haven't seen anything of her for some years, but I've been told she's living somewhere in the Barrows."

For the first time there was a note of sympathy in his voice. "It's a shame for a family to be split up like that. What was the trouble—parents separated, or something?"

I grabbed at this idea and nodded vigorously.

"I'm sorry, Miss, but how can I help? You can't even tell me her name."

"She's supposed to look very much like me . . ." I tried a Rhoda-like gesture and flickered the false eyelashes. "I just thought she might have come into your shop sometimes . . ."

A bona-fide customer had entered, and the grocer at once lost interest in me.

"Sorry Miss." He turned away. "Yes madam, what can I get you?"

Disappointed, but determined not to lose hope, I tried another grocer down the road. I had learned one lesson—buy something first as an introduction. My story was smoother this time and I let my imagination fill in details. In a few minutes I came out holding a quarter of tea, none the wiser.

Soon I had exhausted the grocers in the little shopping area, and I tried butchers, chemists and greengrocers. By now my arms were laden with the things I'd bought. One greengrocer was sympathetic, even presenting me with a carrier bag, but I got nothing out of him. Nobody seemed to have known Rhoda. I got the feeling she must have actually avoided shopping close to home.

My scanty breakfast was a long way off by now. I found a small café, and ordered a ham roll and coffee, and while I was about it, I tried the waitress with questions about Rhoda. Having nothing much to do, she leaned on the table, ready enough to chat.

"Did your sister leave home?" she asked. "Or was you the one?"

I soon realized that her interest was only

idle curiosity. She had nothing to tell me. When I got up to go, I surreptitiously pushed the carrier bag of unwanted purchases out of sight under a chair, hoping to abandon it. But the waitress spotted the wretched thing before I'd got to the door, and was rushing forward helpfully.

Despair began to overtake me. What a ridiculous notion it had been to imagine I could track down an unknown man and pin a murder on him!

I walked back the way I had come, not ready to give up yet, but with real hope extinguished. On a corner there was a small tobacconist's kiosk. I knew Rhoda had been a heavy smoker—she had got through three cigarettes while she was talking to me.

A stout woman sat reading a magazine, seeming to fill her little cubicle completely. She barely looked up at my approach. I bought twenty filter tips I would never smoke, deliberately paying with a pound note to give me an opportunity to launch into my story as she sorted out the change.

She made no effort to be interested. "Never seen her," she snapped, making it

189

clear I was keeping her from the magazine. But I refused to be put off. I had become so hardened by now that even when a man behind me had to reach over my shoulder for his cigarettes, I didn't give way.

"My sister's very like me," I persisted. "And I know she smokes a lot. She must have come here sometimes."

"I never notice what they look like," the woman said indifferently. "I sell them the cigs, that's all."

Dismally, I turned away. What was the use of carrying on with this hopeless quest? I had walked a few vague yards when I heard footsteps hurrying up to me.

"Excuse me, Miss."

A tall man in his mid-thirties, neatly dressed in a smart town suit and bowler hat, was looking down at me.

"Forgive me, but I couldn't help overhearing . . . You see, I was behind you at the cigarette kiosk just now."

I gave him my full attention.

"That business about your sister . . . I think I may know her."

"You do!" My heart gave a triumphant bound.

"As a matter of fact, when I saw you

standing there I thought it was her at first . . ."

"Please," I cut in, "it's terribly important. Where can I find her?"

"Well, when I say I know her, I mean I've seen her around. You know how it is. I've often spotted her coming out of a house just round the corner here. I noticed her specially because . . ." He looked down at me with meaning in his eye. "Well, she's quite a dish—like you!"

"Which house?" I pressed him. "What number is it?"

"I don't know the number, but it's the third house along on the left." He ruminated for a second or two. "Yes, that's it, the third house—the one with a lamp-post right outside."

I gave him a grateful smile. "It's very kind of you."

"Not at all, it's been a pleasure." He raised the bowler politely, and I sensed his eyes still on me as I turned to go.

All my hopes came back with a rush. I dashed down the road, turning as the man had directed. There was the house, the third along, with a lamp-post right outside.

I ran up the half-dozen stone steps and

into the dingy hall. Ahead of me the staircase wound its way out of sight. There
were doors on either side, and faintly I
could hear voices coming from the flat on
the left. I was just about to knock when
the door behind me opened, and I heard
a woman's voice.

"Why hello, Mrs. Willard. I didn't
know you were back."

She *must* mean me—there was no-one
else. I swung round, and saw a stout
woman in a flowered apron, a milk bottle
in her hand. Her expression, only moderately friendly, changed to bewilderment.

"I . . . I'm sorry, but I thought you
were . . . somebody else. From the back
you looked so like her."

"I think that must be my sister. I've
come to see her, but I didn't know which
flat . . ."

The cloud vanished as understanding
took its place. "My word, you *are* like
her."

She didn't volunteer any more, so I had
to ask. "Would you mind telling me where
I can find her?"

"It's the second floor, flat five. But you
won't find your sister there."

I pretended to look surprised. "Is she away, then?"

"Yes, she is. Went off without so much as a word to me, she did. Took all her things. And when I think what I've done for her since she came here . . ."

I cut across the flow of her indignation. "Have you any idea where they've gone?"

"They?" She snorted. "Went off on her own, she did. Left that poor . . . husband of hers flat."

The pieces were beginning to fit together, but I had to discover more. Most important, I wanted to find out if Rhoda's lover had been away from the house on the night she was killed. This neighbour looked as if she might be useful. She was obviously the kind who knew the comings and goings of her fellow tenants.

"I suppose her husband was very upset," I said. "Did he try to follow her?"

Behind me the front door opened. The woman looked up over my shoulder.

"Well now, you can ask him all about it for yourself. Here he is." She spoke to the man who had just come in. "This is Mrs. Willard's sister. She came here looking for her."

Fear struck into me before I turned round. I hadn't expected this—not meeting the man face to face. I had only wanted to establish where he lived; to discover what I could about his movements, so that I could inform the police.

He was a huge man, massively built, with a square, brutish face. He looked capable of anything—even murder. It was difficult to imagine what Rhoda had seen in him. She must have been on her beam ends to take him on for the sake of a few hundred pounds.

Cold grey eyes met mine, unsmiling. The man's face gave no clue to his feelings. He didn't speak. Without another glance at his neighbour, he motioned me to go upstairs.

I hung back. The thought of being alone with him filled me with terror. But I had to go. Not to do so would arouse his suspicion. Reluctantly, I climbed the stairs after him, feeling the stout woman's eyes on my back. I longed to stay in the safety of her presence.

Hastily, I ran through the story in my mind. I must beware of saying anything that flatly contradicted what he might know from Rhoda.

The flat was a two-roomed affair with an alcove of a kitchen curtained off. It was clean enough, though it bore signs of recent neglect. But it was so utterly without character that it possessed about as much comfort as the waiting room of a railway station. In the living-room cheap linoleum covered the floor, with a hearthrug in front of the gas fire. A slot meter stood on view, and a bare minimum of ill-assorted furniture was scattered around. It was obviously a place for birds of passage, not for people to *live* in.

Willard had dumped some paper bags on the table. A potato rolled out on to the floor. He just let it go.

I wasn't asked to sit down.

"Didn't know Rhoda had a sister," he said, looking angry.

"I dare say there's lots of things Rhoda didn't tell you about," I said cautiously.

He grunted, but his immediate suspicions seemed to be lulled.

"There's lots she did tell me, but God alone knows what was true and what wasn't."

"That woman downstairs," I nodded my head in the direction of the hall. "She told me Rhoda had gone off. Is that right?"

"It's right enough. And good riddance! I wouldn't want to clap eyes on that bitch again."

Feeling braver, I probed further. "Surely you don't mean that? After all, she's your wife . . ."

He gave a short bark of a laugh. "My wife! That's a good one."

"You sound as if you hate Rhoda."

"And I've got good reason to! When I met that . . . that *cow*, I'd just come into a bit of money—never mind how. She was broke to the wide, and like a fool I felt sorry for her. The minute she got her paws on the cash she started blewing it."

I had to make a pretence of standing up for my fictitious sister.

"Well, you must have had a hand in it, too."

"And what if I did? It was *my* money, I might remind you. Then when I was laid up, the rotten little bitch cleared off and took what was left with her. I was skint—without a bean."

"Do you know where she went?"

He sneered at me as if that was a mad question. "I told you, she cleared off. She'd hardly leave a forwarding address, would she? No, I've seen the last of her, thank God!"

More sure than ever that I was on the right track, I decided it was time for me to get out. Willard was a dangerous killer.

I picked up my handbag. "Well, sorry you can't help me," I began.

He was looking at me, his early suspicion back in his face. "Why are you so keen to track her down all of a sudden?"

Nervously, I used the bit about not having seen her for years. "A . . . a friend of mine told me she'd spoken to Rhoda a few weeks back, and she said she was living here."

I dared not say any more for fear of giving myself away, but it didn't seem to satisfy him.

It was only now I realized with a sudden shock of dismay that Willard would almost certainly have read about the murder in Dorset. There would be no reason for him to link this with Rhoda's disappearance if he *hadn't* killed her. But now I was convinced that he was the murderer.

My arrival on the scene must appear highly suspicious to him. Was I a policewoman, dolled up to look like Rhoda? Or could I really be her sister, out to see what I could make of the situation? He must have been in a torture of indecision about me.

"Look here," he said suddenly. "I don't want any trouble, see. I have no idea where Rhoda is, and I admit I couldn't care less. So you just be a good girl and don't bother me any more, see."

He more or less pushed me out then. I was glad enough to go, for those last minutes had been pure terror for me. I stumbled my way down the stairs as fast as I could go, determined to head straight for the nearest police station. There was no point in waiting until I got back to Bishop's Cranford. It might even be dangerous. Now that I'd sown suspicion in Willard's mind, he would probably make haste to clear off. It might not be possible to trace him again.

I slammed the front door of the house

shut behind me and stood for a second on the top step, recovering my breath.

A voice spoke in my ear. "How did you get on, dear?"

Leaning out of a window just to one side, elbows planted on the sill, was the stout neighbour. I could see she was settling herself down for a chat. I didn't want to talk to her now, but if I was to be convincing as Rhoda's sister, I had to act through the part. It would still be risky to drop the pretence.

"No luck, I'm afraid," I said morosely. "Mr. Willard hadn't any idea where she might have gone."

"The poor man!" She clucked sympathetically. "She was no good to him, you know. I'm sorry to have to say it, seeing she was your sister and you seem a nice young woman yourself, but she was just out for what she could get. Fancy being so heartless as to leave him just then— knowing how ill he was!"

"Ill? What do you mean?" I thought she might be suggesting Willard was mentally unbalanced, or something which could account for his violence.

"Why, didn't he tell you?" she said,

surprised. "He had an appendix. Very nasty it was, too. They had to rush him off to hospital for an emergency operation." She was full of morbid relish for the gory details. "He was in such pain. They said he wouldn't have lasted another hour."

"In hospital?" I gasped. "But when . . . when did he come out?"

The woman refused to be short-circuited. She shifted her position, making herself more comfortable, her head supported with one hand.

"They came for him . . . let me see . . . must have been about nine in the evening. No, I tell a lie, because my husband had already gone off to his night shift, so it must have been after ten. All that trampling up the stairs and an ambulance outside! Well, I just popped my head out of the door to see what was going on. When they brought that poor man down on a stretcher he was moaning horribly. It gave me quite a turn. And that . . . woman! Sorry as she's your sister, dear. She didn't even trouble herself to come to the door."

"Look," I said urgently, "I'm in a great

hurry. When was it Mr. Willard came out of hospital?"

She looked at me, injured. "Well, wasn't I coming to that? Let me see . . . he went in a fortnight ago last Friday. I know that for a fact because it was my bingo afternoon at the Regal . . ."

"But when did he come out?" I cried bleakly, feeling near to despair.

The woman was getting visibly upset by my interruptions. She regarded me severely. "If it hadn't been for me, that poor man wouldn't have had a single visitor all the time he was in hospital. I went to see him every other day. He was very bitter about *her*, I can tell you—very bitter."

I spoke with restraint, emphasizing each word. "When did he come out? Please tell me."

"Day before yesterday," she snapped.

It just couldn't be true! "Are you quite sure?" I said faintly. "Wasn't it more like a week ago?"

"Am I sure? she says. And it was me and my husband brought him home ourselves—we fetched him in the van.

Day before yesterday, it was, round about four in the afternoon . . ."

I had to hang on to the railings for a minute, because I felt so weak. Then I stumbled away, all my shining hopes of success shattered, pounded to fragments.

The woman was still talking as I turned the corner, but now it sounded like abuse.

11

I HAD failed Mark!

This thought so obsessed me that I can remember nothing of my journey across London from the Barrows back to Paddington. I seem to recall being on a bus at one point, and I must have gone to Euston Square station to collect the things I had left there. But my real memory only returns when I was already on the train heading back to Dorset. Clutched in my arms were my coat, the small case, and the absurd carrier bag full of unwanted items from my shopping expedition. I had carried it with me all this time, unaware.

I was alone in the compartment. Miserably unhappy, I changed back into my own coat and stuffed the white mac into the carrier. I put the bag up on the luggage rack, determined to leave it there. I wanted no more of any of it.

In less than a day I had built hope from almost nothing to a high point of certainty.

Now it was gone, wiped out by the chatter of a garrulous woman.

Mark would guess that my sudden trip to London was prompted by some sort of clue. He would no doubt have been angry that I should run the slightest risk. But at the same time he couldn't have helped hoping I would uncover something useful. Something that would take the spotlight of suspicion off him.

And now I had to go back to him and report utter failure. Worse than that, I had now eliminated one likely suspect.

When I came out of the station at Sherbridge it was only seven in the evening and I thought it likely Mark was still at the factory. But I couldn't face him there. I felt I just wanted to crawl away and hide, and lick my wounds. So I took a taxi home, grateful that in Aunt Frank I had someone who wouldn't fuss.

But when I got to Mead Cottage she was much more concerned than I had expected. She looked at me anxiously, though with no hint of reproach.

"Sit down and tell me about it, Jan dear," she said. She was fiddling over by the welsh dresser, and came across to me with a small glass in her hand. Unexpectedly it was neat whisky, and I spluttered a bit. "You look as if you've had a bad shock," she added.

I told her the whole miserable story, sparing nothing, even when I had to make myself look ridiculous. She took it all in with calm understanding. Aunt Frank offered me nothing in the way of easy comfort. She made no attempt to shield me from reality. I found her prosaic attitude helped me so much more than my mother's fluttering, over-protective concern could ever do.

In a curious way I knew it was just because of my aunt's detachment from life that she could achieve a greater understanding of other people's problems. I suppose most of us are too bound up in our own troubles to take a broader view. I didn't feel the need to elaborate with her, or to exaggerate in the slightest way. She knew exactly what this disappointment meant to me—she knew what I was going through.

Aunt Frank had news of her own which was far worse than anything I had to report. Yet even now she didn't try to spare my feelings by wrapping up her words in cotton wool.

"Mark has been arrested," she said bluntly, pity in her eyes. "The police went to his office this morning, and took him with them to the station."

I looked up at her dumbly, too horrified to speak.

"They want to talk to you as well, my dear. Of course, that's only to be expected —they'll know about you and Mark."

"Me and Mark?" I whispered, still feeling dazed. Did they know everything, then?

"How you two feel about one another, I mean," Aunt Frank said gently. "It's just a matter of routine, all this questioning."

I wanted to go to Mark right away, I wanted to tell the police how utterly wrong they were even to *suspect* that he could have murdered Rhoda. But my aunt insisted it would be no use going to Sherbridge police station tonight.

"They won't let you see him, Jan. Not until they've had a chance to question you. Wait until they come here tomorrow, and ask then if you can visit Mark."

The news of the arrest was a dreadful shock, yet underneath I realized I was not really surprised. I could understand that the police must regard this as an open and shut case. Why should they look any further?

But the next morning I was to discover that the case against Mark was even more formidable than I had feared.

Sergeant Hayes called to see me soon after eleven. His face was full and fleshy, weatherbeaten, with bushy eyebrows. He had the appearance of a farmer about him more than a policeman. His heavy tweed suit and soft trilby gave him a friendly, neighbourly look as he came in. He knocked out his pipe on his heel, putting it into his jacket pocket as if reluctantly.

Apparently he knew Aunt Frank well, and he shook her warmly by the hand. Then he turned to me with an agreeable smile.

"Good morning, Miss Prior."

I couldn't bring myself to take his outstretched hand and I gave him a cool nod. I was trembling nervously from head to foot. Aunt Frank asked the sergeant to sit down while she herself sat firmly on the settle, making it quite clear that she intended to stay in the room. She pulled me down beside her.

Sergeant Hayes lowered himself rather gingerly into a windsor chair by the fireplace. His hand hovered at his back, suggesting that he suffered from sciatica. He relaxed with a sigh.

"Well now, Miss," he began. "I'd like to have a little chat with you, if you don't mind."

I did mind. I minded like hell! This man had been responsible for putting Mark behind bars, and I resented him fiercely. To be fair, I believe he got no pleasure out of what he was doing. His whole attitude spoke of sorrow more than of satisfaction. I was aware that he was going out of his way to be gentle in handling me.

"Your aunt told me you had taken a trip to London. Thought you'd do a bit of detective work on our doubtful friend Willard, eh?"

Instantly I was jerked out of my mood of numb resignation. How could he possibly know what I had been doing in London? I was sure Aunt Frank wouldn't have told him that—in any case she hadn't known about Willard before I had arrived back last night.

"I suppose you're surprised that we know?" The sergeant gave me a slow smile. "The police got there just after you had left. They heard all about the young woman who had been doing a sister act, so we didn't have to be very clever to put two and two together." His official tone relaxed still further until he sounded almost fatherly. "Now why did you go and do that? Why not leave it to us?"

"But you didn't seem to take any notice when Mark ... when Mr. Galbraith suggested it could be a man from his wife's past. He told me so himself."

"But of course we took notice—we take notice of everything. It would have been just the same if Mr. Galbraith hadn't suggested it. We should certainly have enquired into the victim's past life. As a matter of fact, in this case it wasn't particularly difficult, anyway. We found a cloakroom ticket in her bag, and through that we unearthed all her possessions. They told us a great deal about the young lady."

I just couldn't stay still. I jumped to my

feet, and then sat down again almost at once over by the table.

"It all makes me look rather silly," I said, eyes fixed on my shoes.

"On the contrary, I think such concern about Mr. Galbraith is to be commended. And anyway you beat us to it, which was clever of you. I'd like to know what gave you the clue?"

I kept silent. I was trying to think what I could say without giving too much away.

The detective solved my difficulty for me. He leaned forward in his chair, crinkling up his intelligent eyes.

"I might as well tell you that it's perfectly obvious you must have seen Rhoda . . . er . . . Willard before she died. Otherwise you couldn't have impersonated her so accurately."

In the end I told him everything about Rhoda's visit. There seemed no point in trying to conceal it any longer.

He sat very still, listening to my story. Once or twice when I became confused, he would ask a question, but apart from that he didn't interrupt. When I had finished he shook his head sadly.

"You could have saved yourself all the

trouble of going to London, and a bitter disappointment, if only you'd known . . ."

"Known?" I cried. "Known what?"

"That we already had evidence it was someone local. You see, Mr. Galbraith's boat was used to take the body out to sea —the signs are quite definite. For one thing we found a mackintosh hat which matched her coat. Fortunately for us, the murderer wasn't careful enough about weighting the body, so it floated to the surface. Otherwise we'd never have found her."

"That doesn't prove it was Mr. Galbraith," I said defiantly.

He nodded, acknowledging the fairness of my comment. "But it all adds up. Only a local man would have known enough about the state of the tides at Mulstead Cove. It's quite tricky getting a boat out safely, and remember—this was after dark."

I was going to cut in again, but he held up his hand. "That's not all, I'm afraid. In the back of Mr. Galbraith's car we found his mother's cheque for five hundred pounds. It was torn up and stuffed in the ashtray, out of sight."

It looked as if the police had been a shade too clever. At last I saw a tiny chink of light. "But that's ridiculous! Mr. Galbraith would never use the ashtray in the *back* of his own car. In any case, why should he put the cheque there at all?"

The sergeant was not worried by his attack. "The body had to be moved down to the beach, you see." He regarded me steadily. "Now suppose Mr. Galbraith discovered the cheque on the body whilst he was getting it into the car. He would want to destroy it in order to conceal his motive for the killing. What more natural than to put the cheque in the ashtray, and then forget to destroy it later?"

Horrified by this mounting circumstantial evidence, I floundered around, desperately trying to find something to discount it. I recalled that Mark had been openly asking about Rhoda at the village pub on the day after the murder. "He would hardly have done that if he'd been guilty, would he?"

Sergeant Hayes shook his head. "It could just as easily have been done deliberately, as a cover up." His eyes were so kind, but his words struck chill into my heart. "I'm sorry, Miss Prior, believe me I am. I can understand your loyalty—it's only natural you can't bring yourself to accept that the man you love is capable of murder. But I'm afraid my experience tells me that *anyone* can come to the point of killing when they are driven by desperation. I've known Mark Galbraith since he was a boy. I like him, and I admire him for what he's been doing for his uncle. But all the liking in the world won't colour my appraisal of the evidence. I can't let it. It isn't my job to judge a man—that's for someone else. I have to dig out facts, and facts can't be ignored."

He stopped speaking, and there was silence in the room. I wanted to scream out against his coldly logical arguments. I think I would have done, but Aunt Frank got up and came over to where I was sitting by the table. She put a hand on my shoulder, and somehow, because she was so sparing of gestures of affection, it was enormously comforting at the moment.

I knew the sergeant was wrong. For all his experience and psychology, he was utterly wrong. Whatever he might say, I knew Mark was not capable of murder. I *knew* it. As much as I had ever known anything. As well as I knew that night would follow day.

I remembered how we had clung together, Mark and I, that first and last time. The barriers between us were down, and Mark was free to tell me that he loved me. By then, it had been already too late; fresh barriers were in position. But nothing could destroy that moment for me. It had been unique and wonderful; it had brought great joy as well as great sadness. And if I had not known before, it told me that Mark could not possibly have been Rhoda's murderer.

How could I tell all this to a police officer? How could I explain that love can be right, and cold logic wrong? How could I possibly convince him that all his careful deduction was wasted, set at naught by the intuition of an untrained mind?

It was difficult to understand why this astute detective could not see that Lady Galbraith was an equally likely suspect. With the knowledge that Willard was not the killer, my old suspicions of Mark's mother returned with greater force than ever. Everything fitted. She was a strong woman, mentally and physically. If sufficiently roused—and anything threatening her fanatical respectability was enough for that—she would be perfectly capable of drastic action. She had the strength to move the body, and the knowledge to sail Mark's boat out to sea. In the old days she had done plenty of sailing.

It looked as if Mark was making no attempt to clear himself because it would mean suspicion falling on his mother. I became more and more certain that he was deliberately shielding her from a charge of murder.

I longed to divulge what I suspected. To tell about Lady Galbraith's strange behaviour the day after Rhoda's visit; her utter certainty that Rhoda—a blackmailer—would never return to trouble Mark again. But I couldn't do this. If Mark was shielding his mother, it was *his* decision. He had always shielded her and defended her against criticism. He knew what she was, and he accepted that she had many faults. But she was his mother, and he loved and respected her despite them.

I seethed with loathing for Lady Galbraith—a woman who could allow her son to accept the consequences of her actions. What was this obsession with respectability if she even could abandon Mark in face of its demands?

The scene in Aunt Frank's sitting-room was like a tableau. Three silent figures. My aunt standing, her hand still upon my shoulder. Myself sitting at the table, hopeless and despairing. The sergeant leaning forward watching me, his big hands spread out on his knees. His face was full of concern.

At length I broke a silence that seemed to have lasted an age.

"Have you . . . charged Mr. Galbraith yet?"

The sergeant spoke softly. "Yes. He appeared before the magistrate first thing this morning, and has been remanded in custody."

"Can I see him, please?"

His glance took me in, summing me up before he replied. "I don't see why not."

"Oh thank you." I was grateful to him, as though he was giving me a present.

"Anyway, we shall want a statement from you—about Rhoda . . . Willard's visit here. Come back with me now, and kill two . . . attend to both matters at the same time."

I didn't know what I should say to Mark, for there was nothing I could do to help him now. My failure in London would be a bitter blow, if he was living in hopes that I had unearthed some evidence to clear him.

Yet had he really believed in my theory? Was he ever convinced that Rhoda's lover had killed her? Or had he only clutched wildly at this straw of hope to keep at bay the fear that his mother was the real murderer?

Nevertheless, I longed to see him. I felt I couldn't wait another minute.

"Thank you, Sergeant Hayes," I replied. "I'll get ready at once."

12

I WAS shown into a small shabby room, and asked to wait.

Sherbridge police station was old and grimy, tucked away in a back street. The room I was in looked depressingly on to a courtyard. I noticed the window was heavily barred.

I wondered where Mark was, and whether he knew that I was here.

The friendly Sergeant Hayes seemed to have deserted me. After a few minutes on my own, a casual young man strolled in and introduced himself as Detective-Constable Harvey.

"If you'd like to give me your statement," he said, his voice Dorset-burred.

In a way his impersonal attitude helped me to give a coherent story. Perhaps that was why Sergeant Hayes had chosen him. It took nearly half-an-hour. The constable wrote what I told him in painstaking longhand, and when I had read it through and signed it, I was left cooling my heels again.

The near silence became almost unbearable. I could hear faint voices outside, a door closing, echoing footsteps that always stopped short of the room I was in.

At last the voices and the footsteps came right up and the door opened. Mark was shown in, and as I jumped up to go to him, I saw a uniformed young policeman take up guard just beside the door.

The sinister implication of his presence restrained my impetuous rush towards Mark.

We stood there, looking unhappily at one another. Over Mark's shoulder I could see the policeman at the door shuffling his feet, gazing beyond us into space.

"How are you, Mark?"

He came forward, his arms outstretched, and held me for a moment, a hand on each shoulder.

"Jan, it's good to see you."

But I was hardly listening. I was shocked by the look of defeat about him, as though all hope had been finally abandoned.

We sat down facing one another across the small table. Our hands rested on its surface, hovering, wanting to touch, but held back by the knowledge that we were observed.

"How are you, Mark?" I repeated.

"Me? Oh, I'm all right. It's not so bad, really. I'm being treated very well." If this was for the benefit of the gaoler, his impassive face showed nothing. Whether he was taking in what we said there was no way of knowing.

"I . . . I wish you weren't mixed up in all this business." Mark spread out his hands, to cover the whole sordid mess. "But what could I do? They knew well enough that Rhoda had been to see you. Hayes told me so himself."

"Don't worry about it, Mark. They were bound to find out—Aunt Frank said so all along. And anyway, I have nothing to hide. Neither of us have. How can they possibly imagine that you might have . . . done it? It must be obvious that you wouldn't do anything like that."

Surely the policeman at the door must be taking note of what we said? Surely he would report what he heard, and his superiors would realize that Mark must be innocent?

Mark cut across these foolish thoughts.

"I heard you had gone to London," he said. "What was it all about, Jan?"

I told him the whole story. He showed no surprise when I explained that Rhoda's lover could not possibly have killed her—only concern that I should have exposed myself to such risks. He shook his head in exasperation.

"It was sweet of you, Jan, to try to help me, but you really shouldn't have gone. That man might have harmed you, hating Rhoda so much and thinking you were her sister."

"But I had to try, Mark."

He nodded. "You must promise me you won't attempt anything like that again. There's nothing you can do for me now, Jan. There's nothing anyone can do."

If a tiny doubt had remained that Mark really believed his mother had killed Rhoda, it disappeared now. He had given up the fight, and there could only be one reason for that. I knew he wasn't guilty, so he must be protecting the one who was.

"Mark," I said urgently. "It isn't fair for you to take the blame."

He looked straight at me, and I knew we understood one another.

"No!" he said emphatically. Then he lowered his tone. "Perhaps it isn't fair, Jan. But there is nothing to be done about it. All the evidence points to me, and no amount of raking up the past will alter that."

It was a warning against any wild idea of implicating his mother. He wouldn't allow her to be dragged in, and that was final. Whatever the consequences, Mark would accept them for his mother's sake.

There was silence between us. Mark had his elbows on the table, his head bent forward to his hands. Faintly I could hear the ticking of his wrist-watch.

"Look, Jan," he said awkwardly at last. "I don't want you to get any more mixed up in this business than you already are. There isn't anything you can do, you must understand that."

"But Mark . . . !"

"No," he said sadly, "no 'buts' Jan. You just go home to Kutain as soon as you are able to, and forget about all this. Perhaps it was a pity we met a second time. Until we did, we were able to believe it was over between us."

"Mark! I couldn't just go back and leave you like this."

My heart cried out in protest against this new Mark, this man with a beaten look. Mark was a fighter. One only had to think of what he had done for his uncle's business to know that. Yet here he was, giving up, allowing events to overwhelm him.

He startled me by suddenly standing up. I couldn't bear it that already I must go. I wanted to stay with him, to talk and plan. But what was there to talk about? What was there to plan?

"We'd better say good-bye now, Jan," Mark said in a quiet controlled voice.

Miserably I got up too. "I'll see you again soon, Mark," I promised.

He nodded. "Good-bye, Jan," he said huskily, holding out a formal hand.

I tried to sound bright. "Till next time."

He bit his lip. Blinking, I could barely control the tears in my eyes.

"Jan!" My name was like a strangled cry. I swung round. Mark was standing there beside the table. He looked unutterably sad, holding the back of his chair as if he needed its support.

His lips outlined the words, the words I
had longed for, and never heard until it
was too late.

"*I love you.*"

I stumbled out of the room, choking
back my tears. Perhaps after all the young
policeman was not so completely impersonal as he had seemed. He couldn't look
at me as he held the door open. He gazed
down intently at his boots, his ears scarlet.

A police car took me back to Bishop's
Cranford. At first the two patrol men,
anxious to be kind, tried to make polite
conversation. I was too numbed to find
words to answer them, and the remainder
of the journey passed in silence.

I wanted to get to my bedroom, feeling
I just couldn't hang on to self-control any
longer. But Aunt Frank met me in the
front garden.

"Jan, we've got a visitor."

A visitor was the last thing I wanted just
then.

"Who . . . who is it?"

"Come and see!"

Wondering a little I followed her into
the cottage.

"Sally!"

She stood there looking just as she had always done—smiling and enormously friendly. And now there was the added confidence that a successful marriage puts upon a woman. But I noticed there was also an anxious quality in her expression, a certain diffidence, as if she were not entirely sure of my reaction to her presence.

I managed a smile. "Hallo, Sally."

"It's lovely to see you again, Jan," she said, running forward and embracing me.

It was five years since we had met. Normally I would have been delighted to see her again, but now . . . We stood there looking at each other, neither of us knowing quite what to say.

"Are you here for long?" I asked.

"No." She looked away uneasily. "Actually, I've only just popped down for the day. That's why I came straight round. I've got to start back to Worcester this afternoon." She hesitated again. "Jan, I've heard all about your trouble through Aunt Dolly. I'm dreadfully sorry."

"Do you know that Mark has been arrested?"

She nodded. "Yes, that's really why . . ." She was looking guilty, as if ashamed.

Aunt Frank clearly decided it was time to leave us alone. "I'd better go and do something about lunch. You're sure you won't join us, Sally?"

"Thanks, but I can't. I really mustn't stay more than a few minutes. Aunt Dolly is expecting me back."

When my aunt had gone I looked at Sally. "What was it you were going to say just now?"

"Well, Uncle Lionel's been so much better lately," she began with a rush. "The news about Mark would set him right back."

"I know," I said sadly. "It is dreadful, but I don't see how we can keep it from him for long."

"I thought I could try," said Sally. She was looking positively hangdog by now. "I . . . I'm taking them both back home with me. I suggested it as a little holiday, and they liked the idea. I thought in Worcester we could manage to conceal things from Uncle—for a while, at least.

To give him more time to get his strength back."

Now it was out! I didn't wonder what Sally had found it so difficult to tell me.

"So you're clearing off and leaving Mark to his fate?" I said bitterly. "You're all very sorry, of course, but you want no part of it."

"Jan, it's not like that," Sally protested. "If there was anything we could do for Mark . . ."

"You could stand by him," I shouted. "He's your cousin. You could show you believed in him. Mark gave up his career when your uncle had his stroke, and came down here to rescue the business. But now that *he's* in trouble, the Buxtons can't run away fast enough."

Sally stood for a minute with her head bowed. When she looked up I could see there were tears in her eyes. She spoke very quietly.

"Mark has always been a very special person to me, Jan, and I'm terribly conscious of how much we owe him. He's been absolutely marvellous. But all he has done for us will have been wasted if Uncle Lionel should have another stroke now. So far, Aunt Dolly has been able to keep it from Uncle, but it's been difficult. And she wouldn't be able to explain why Mark couldn't come to see him every day or so, as usual. Uncle Lionel thinks the world of Mark. I really believe it would kill him if he discovered what had happened."

Sally put out her hands in a helpless gesture. "I know it must look as if we are running out on Mark, but it's not that— honestly Jan! I'm just trying to think of what's best for Uncle. It's not as if there is anything we can really do to help Mark, is there?"

I closed my eyes, bitterly ashamed of my outburst, those cruel words torn from me in my misery. I knew that I had been desperately unfair in accusing Sally of selfishness. She was only thinking of saving her uncle from the dangerous consequences of shock. In my own distress I had forgotten that Lionel Buxton's life still hung in the balance. That a shock might be more than his tremulous heart could bear. Mark would understand what Sally was trying to do. Mark would be glad. I strove against the sensation that she and her uncle and aunt were running away when Mark most needed help. There was no help they could give. There was no help anybody could give.

Except for one selfish bigoted woman living in an ivory castle of pride . . .

"I'm sorry, Sally. It was unforgivable of me."

"That's all right, Jan," she said, her quick warm smile returning. "I think I'd have felt just the same in your shoes."

Through our tears we looked at each other, and found again the understanding we had shared in the past. I realized how wrong it was of me to imagine I was the only one who cared about Mark. Sally and the Buxtons loved him also, and they too were suffering. If Lionel Buxton learned the truth just now . . . It didn't bear thinking about.

I tried to put real enthusiasm into my voice. "It's a very good idea for you to take your uncle and aunt back to Worcester. I'm sure it's the best thing you could possibly do, Sally."

"Thank you, Jan."

"Have you brought the baby with you?" I went on, forcing myself to make conversation. "I'm longing to see him."

But she hadn't, and I was glad. It would have been difficult to have cooed over a baby in my present mood. And too difficult not to have shown my envy of Sally's happy state.

"Paul's mother is looking after Kevin for me," she said. "But perhaps you could come to Worcester for a weekend before you . . . you go back to Kutain . . ."

Sally's invitation trailed off doubtfully. I guessed she was realizing that if I were to visit her home, it would scarcely be possible to keep the conversation away from Mark. Her mention of my return to Kutain cast a further gloom upon me. After the trial I should have to go home. Even though I could do nothing for Mark by staying in England, I still hated the thought of being so far away from him.

To change a painful subject I said, "What does Derek think about you taking your uncle and aunt back to Worcester?" It struck me that Derek might not be so keen on the idea, since it would mean he'd be left to fend for himself.

Sally shrugged. "He'll just have to lump it. It won't do that brother of mine any harm at all to discover what it's like having to cope on your own. I bet he's finding that out right now at the factory."

"You mean now that Mark isn't there?" I said, a little surprised at her critical tone.

Sally eyed me. "Well yes," she admitted. "It's no use pretending, is it? Poor Derek always imagined he would inherit the business, of course. When we were kids he used to boast about how he would change things. He had visions of big expansion, with a chromium-plated head office in London. And all the time it was glaringly obvious that he just wasn't up to administration of any kind."

I said nothing. There seemed nothing to say.

"It must have been a blow to Derek when they called in Mark to take over," Sally went on. "But really it was a wonderful idea. And if he could only see it, Derek himself will be better off in the end if the firm is thriving . . . I mean, he *would* have been . . ."

Whatever we said came back to the same terrible dead end. Mark's arrest loomed over us, dominating everything.

"If only Rhoda had never come into our lives!" Sally exclaimed with a sigh.

"She brought us nothing but trouble. Remember how gone on her Derek was in the old days? And then she went and ditched him for Mark."

Aunt Frank had come into the room to lay the table. "That's news to me," she said, as she put the tray down. "There was something between Rhoda and Derek, then?"

I nodded glumly, but Sally brightened, and I knew she was glad to be released from the strain of making conversation with me.

"Oh yes, Miss Prior. It was quite an affair. It began the summer Jan was here and went on for a long time, blowing hot and blowing cold. She treated him abominably, but Derek was utterly hooked and would always go running whenever she deigned to smile on him. Then suddenly Rhoda decided to make a play for Mark when he was home one vacation. That was the end of my brother as far as she was concerned."

"Well, perhaps it's just as well for Derek," Aunt Frank said thoughtfully. "Considering how the girl turned out."

It was a relief when Sally got up to

leave. Again we stood looking at each other for a moment, searching for words.

"Oh Jan . . . !"

She flung herself at me in a quick embrace, then turned on her heels and hurried away. I stood where I was, feeling utterly exhausted, while Aunt Frank went with Sally as far as the gate.

That afternoon I settled down to write to my parents. It was incredibly difficult. I tore up sheet after sheet of notepaper before Aunt Frank came to my rescue by suggesting that she should send a letter ahead of mine. I accepted her offer gratefully. It would be much better for Mother and Dad to read her concise appraisal of the facts before they received my distressed and probably incoherent version.

With the Buxtons gone I had even less to help me fill the empty days ahead. I would have given a lot to be terribly busy, my mind so crowded that I had no time left over to think.

The next morning I went for a long solitary walk, but the beauty of the Dorset countryside meant nothing to me when

Mark was shut away, unable to enjoy it too.

I returned home as I had set out, through the field path that led off Church Lane. I was avoiding going through the village. Now even more than before, I shrank from meeting people who would recognize me. Above everything else I was terrified that I might run into Mark's mother. It was something I couldn't face.

I had seen nothing of Lady Galbraith since the morning Mark had taken me to *Elgin House* and she had tried to deny having seen Rhoda. Mark and I hadn't known then that Rhoda had been killed, her body thrown into the sea.

It was one of the afternoons when Mrs. Bird came to do the cleaning at Mead Cottage. She arrived with her shopping basket bulging as usual, and with an air of excitement only very thinly veiled. Mrs. Bird was an inveterate gossip, and I suppose she must have regarded it as a stroke of good fortune to be employed at two houses so closely connected with a murder. It was obvious that she expected me to be ready to discuss it, and she was greatly disappointed when I refused to cooperate. But unwillingly, I found myself listening when she began to chatter about Lady Galbraith. What she had to say astonished me.

"Her Ladyship is carrying on just as if nothing had happened," Mrs. Bird chirruped. "She was on at me this morning to have the house just so for a committee meeting she's got there this afternoon—Friends of the Hospital or something." She gave me a doubtful glance. "I suppose you've got to admire her—in a way."

I couldn't stop myself from asking, "Do you know if she's been to visit her son?"

"I know for a fact she hasn't," Mrs. Bird replied, and I caught the criticism in her voice. "She's not so much as mentioned his name either—not once. She used to be that proud of Mr. Mark, she'd never stop talking about him—even to me. It was always 'look what my son has given me' or 'I'll ask my son to see about it, Mrs. Bird'. But now—well, it's almost as if she hadn't got a son any more. Even though he's a murderer, you'd expect his own mother to stand up for him—it's only human nature, after all." She caught her breath. "Poor Mr. Mark! It's dreadful! And him such a nice young man, too."

I turned and fled up the narrow stairs to my bedroom, to hide the tears that once again were starting to flow.

I found I was touched by Mrs. Bird's sympathy for Mark. Even though, like everyone else, she believed he had murdered Rhoda, she seemed to have more feeling for him than the mother who could so ruthlessly dismiss him from her life. My hatred of Lady Galbraith was threatening to saturate my whole being like an insidious poison.

I was due to visit Mark again the following day, but in the morning there was a letter from him.

Wondering, impatient, I ripped open the envelope. Inside was just a single sheet of paper.

Jan, my darling, *it read.* Thank you for coming to see me—thank you for believing in me. Knowing that you do helps me more than I can say.

But we have to face facts. There is no way out for me. No way that I could take.

Please try to understand, Jan, that it is better for us not to meet again. Visiting me here can bring nothing but pain to you. And when you are gone I am filled with longing.

Good-bye, Jan, my dearest love. I shall always be thinking of you.

13

"CAN I leave the apple sauce to you, Jan?" Aunt Frank's voice was unusually brisk and businesslike.

I picked out some apples from the vegetable rack and began to peel them in a desultory sort of way. I couldn't take any interest at all in food. Eating was just something I did at intervals in order to keep alive—and even that seemed hardly worth while as things were. With Mark facing trial for murder, and the evidence so heavily piled against him, life itself seemed of little value.

Unlike the usual scratch meals at Mead Cottage, we were preparing an elaborate Sunday lunch. Aunt Frank had invited Derek Buxton. For some reason she had seemed hell-bent on the idea of having him. I had overheard her jollying him on the phone, bulldozing through his obvious reluctance.

"I simply won't take no for an answer,"

she had declared, sounding almost as arch as my mother would have done.

I began to wonder if her motive was simply the kindly one of wanting to offer him hospitality now his family was away. Could it be that after all she had turned into a match-maker and was intent on pushing Derek and I together?

I could well imagine Mrs. Buxton conniving with her. Derek's aunt made no secret of her hopes in that direction—she had often dropped little sighing hints to the effect that we would make an ideal pair. Perhaps Aunt Frank had decided that Derek would help take my mind off Mark.

I liked Derek well enough; he was good company. But I had no time to spare for him now. I was locked up with my grief just as Mark was by the bars of his prison cell. All my thoughts were turned on him in a ceaseless, feverish quest for proof of his innocence.

But it was a useless quest. How could I hope to prove him innocent when he himself was so determined to be found guilty? How could I do anything to save him when his one thought was to shield the real murderer—his mother?

Aunt Frank was displaying a hidden and unsuspected talent for cookery. We were to have stuffed roast pork; melon to begin and a sherry trifle to finish. She had even ordered a couple of bottles of dinner wine, something she didn't normally bother to have in the house.

The gate-legged table had been laid with conscious elegance. The whole lavish display seemed unnecessary to me, even a bit cruel. How could Aunt Frank expect me to enthuse over a social occasion in the present circumstances?

I did the best I could. I remembered how kind she had always been to me in the past, and I tried not to spoil her party. When Derek arrived we stood around amiably sipping sherry, everything in the kitchen apparently under perfect control. The warm sun shone in through the open french windows, and old Felix was asleep, curled up on the stone step outside. The world looked deceptively peaceful that Sunday morning—I felt I was being a traitor to Mark.

Derek was far from being at ease. He appeared very subdued, with none of his usual swagger. I imagine that anyway he would have felt uncomfortable as Aunt Frank's guest. In spite of her friendship with his uncle and aunt, I had hardly ever heard her exchange more than an odd word with Derek—they really had nothing in common at all. We made small talk about innocuous things. After a few minutes Aunt Frank went out to the kitchen to dish up, and Derek began to ask me a string of questions about Kutain. He seemed as anxious as I was to keep the conversation away from the real and tragic present.

At the table Aunt Frank carved the joint inexpertly. Then, as she was offering Derek roast potatoes, she said suddenly, "You must be finding life rather busy at the moment—I mean, having to do Mark's job as well as your own?"

Derek looked embarrassed. "Well, I do my best, you know."

"I suppose you are pretty well used to Mark's methods by now?"

It was a tactless remark, and Derek reacted as I would have expected. "*Mark's* methods?" he exclaimed. Then, making a visible effort not to show his annoyance, he went on mildly, "We developed the ideas between us. Mark and I have made a lot of necessary changes since Uncle Lionel was taken ill."

"Poor Mark!" Aunt Frank said, shaking her grey head. "Being accused of a murder he didn't do."

"Didn't do?" Derek burst out. I too was surprised by her positive statement. Aunt Frank had been kind and understanding in her attitude to Mark, but she had not before made such an utterly dogmatic pronouncement of her belief in his innocence.

Her eyes widened as she looked across the table at Derek. "*You* don't think he did it, surely?" she asked.

Derek flushed. "It . . . it was just that you seemed so certain." He glanced at me, uncomfortably. "I mean . . . naturally nobody wants to think . . . But then the poor devil did have good cause to . . ."

I was already so frozen inside that, though I heard what he was saying, I didn't react in any way. What was it to me that Derek obviously thought Mark was guilty? Everybody else did, too.

Except Aunt Frank, apparently.

"You mean," she was saying to Derek

calmly. "You mean that he wanted to be free to marry again?"

Derek flicked another perplexed glance at me. "Isn't it obvious?" he muttered. "Er . . . couldn't we drop the subject—it can't be very pleasant for Jan . . ."

Aunt Frank ignored his warning. She seemed oblivious of the effect the conversation might be having on me. In a level voice she said, "Of course, it's perfectly possible that Margaret Galbraith is the one the police should have arrested."

"*No!*" Derek's vehement protest swung my attention back to him. He was almost shouting. "It isn't possible! Aunt Margaret! It's unthinkable!"

"Why do you say that?" Aunt Frank was at her most analytical, just as if she was discussing a matter utterly unconnected with any of us. "If you consider it for a moment, Derek, you'll see she had the motive. Having in mind her rigid ideas about her place in society, Rhoda's return would have meant a scandal beyond bearing. And she certainly had the opportunity, too. She is a strong woman, remember."

Derek and I were both staring at her in

confusion. I was astonished that Aunt Frank should so accurately have described my own interpretation of Rhoda's death. Out of loyalty to Mark, I had said nothing to her about my suspicions concerning Lady Galbraith.

Derek, however, was not only astonished, but horrified. I couldn't understand it. He had accepted the idea of his *cousin's* guilt readily enough, so why was he so violently rejecting the suggestion that his *aunt* should have killed Rhoda?

Aunt Frank seemed unaware of the consternation she was causing. Tranquilly she helped herself to another spoonful of peas.

"I was surprised when the police arrested Mark," she went on. "What does their evidence amount to that doesn't apply with equal force to his mother? Is there a single thing that points inevitably to Mark?"

"Well," Derek burst out. "Taking the body out to sea in the dinghy, for one thing."

"Lady Galbraith could sail that boat, too. She used to do a good deal of sailing until a few years ago."

"But you can't believe she was responsible," Derek insisted. "Anyway, what about the cheque found in Mark's car?"

"Anyone could have planted it there." Aunt Frank shrugged her shoulders in mild contempt. "I don't suppose Mark locks his car every time he parks it. What is much more significant to my mind is that the police found no trace at all that Rhoda's body had ever been in Mark's car."

"But why should they? I mean, Rhoda was strangled. It wasn't as if she was bleeding from open wounds, or anything like that."

Aunt Frank reached for the bottle of burgundy and refilled her glass. She pushed the bottle over towards Derek, but he appeared not to notice. "Really Derek," she said. "You don't seem to know much about modern police methods."

"What do you mean—modern methods?"

"Why, when their back room boys get down to it, the police can dig out the most fantastic evidence. I heard of one case . . ." She sat back in her chair, settling down to a story. It all seemed so unbelievably heartless to me. "A man was killed on the road by a hit and run driver somewhere in Kent, and the forensic people were able to prove that a human hair found caught by the rim of the head-lamp on the suspected car came from the victim's head."

Derek looked at my aunt in silence for a moment. "That's different," he said slowly. "A violent accident like that. It's quite another matter from putting a dead body in a car."

"Don't you believe it." Aunt Frank was shaking her head. "Even then there would almost certainly be *some* trace. Perhaps just a tiny fibre from her clothes—a shred of wool rubbed off when she was dragged into the car. The slightest thing like that would be enough. And then, of course, she may have been alive, and got in—which-ever car it was—herself, and a quarrel developed afterwards. In that case there would probably be fingerprints."

Again Derek stared at her. The food on his plate, and mine too, was congealing, cold and almost untouched. But Aunt Frank didn't notice.

At last Derek spoke again. "But all this is sheer. . . supposition."

My aunt started clearing away the plates and vegetable dishes. In a daze I got up to help her. At the door she paused. "You're right, Derek," she said. "It is only supposition. But I have an idea the truth will come out in the way I've suggested. I don't believe Mark killed Rhoda. It could have been his mother, or it could have been someone else. We'll just have to wait and see if I'm not right."

To my great relief Aunt Frank let the subject drop then. All through the dessert she chatted brightly about radio personalities she had met. She could be a wonderful raconteur when she liked, but the display was wasted on her present audience. I was too unhappy to take any pleasure from her dry wit, and Derek seemed to be preoccupied.

It was barely three o'clock when he announced that he had to be going.

"Got such a lot to do," he muttered apologetically.

Aunt Frank didn't press him to stay. "You must come again soon," she said. "It's been so nice having you." Then, presumably because I hadn't made any contribution to the conversation for a very long time, she added rather sharply, "Hasn't it, Jan?"

"Oh . . . oh yes," I said hurriedly. "I . . . I've enjoyed it."

That was a patent lie, but it was necessary to go through the social niceties, however mechanically.

The dishes were piled in the kitchen, and when Derek had gone we washed up together. Aunt Frank, abstracted as ever, was humming *The Blue Danube* to herself.

At length I ventured, "I didn't realize you were so convinced of Mark's innocence."

"Didn't you, dear? But then, I've never thought anything else."

I stood there, stupidly wiping and rewiping a tiny coffee cup, half-hopeful and yet half reconciled to helpless misery. "Isn't there *anything* we can do, Aunt Frank?"

She patted my hand with her wet one. "Give it a little more time, Jan. You mustn't give up hope."

When we had finished I took a folding

chair into the garden and settled in the sunshine, pretending to read the Sunday paper. But I had learned in the last few days that I could settle to nothing, that my mind would always revert to agonizing over Mark.

My aunt didn't join me in the garden as usual. When after ten minutes or so she did appear, she was dressed to go out, a coat pulled on over her blouse and skirt.

"I'm just off for a little walk, Jan dear." She didn't suggest I should join her, and I was glad, really. It suited my mood better to be left quite alone just now.

As I had done a hundred times already, I went over every tiny aspect of the case against Mark. Again I dissected Rhoda's visit to me, searching minutely for some tiny shred of evidence that would lead in a new direction. But I always came back to the fact that the only credible alternative to Mark was his mother. I *knew* it couldn't be Mark, so it had to be Lady Galbraith.

And there was nothing I could do about it. There was nothing anybody could do, despite Aunt Frank's cheerful optimism.

To Aunt Frank a walk meant several miles of plodding over the hills, so I was surprised when half-an-hour later I saw her striding up the lane.

She went straight to the garage. I watched her, astonished.

"I've just thought of something I must see to in Sherbridge," she explained.

She had forgotten what day it was, of course! That was so like her. "None of the shops will be open today," I reminded her gently.

She looked round at me, surprised. "No dear, of course they won't. It's Sunday."

Her car never would start easily—the penalty of her neglect. When at last she got it going, she backed out and paused on the short gravel drive for a moment.

"I don't expect I'll be very long, but carry on with your tea if I should be delayed."

She went off to a grinding of gears. Aunt Frank was a bad driver. It was one of the few things she couldn't do well.

I had an afternoon with no interruptions before me, no callers expected. I had wanted solitude, and yet now I found my aloneness intolerable. I jumped up and walked aimlessly round the little garden. It was a mistake to open the door of the shed. The sight of the rusty bicycle standing there brought a fresh storm of tears.

I stumbled back to the cottage, up the stairs to my room, and threw myself down on the bed, filled with hopeless stifling despair. There was no way out for Mark. And that meant there was no way out for me, either.

The future was in deep shadow. I dared not let my thoughts wander ahead to the trial that was to come.

I thought of today, only today. I longed to see Mark again, and yet I was glad that he was strong enough to keep us apart. There was nothing to say now. I could offer him no hope. I could only take him my misery to add to his own. I could only cause him new agony of mind in knowing how desperate I felt.

The silence was shattered by a furious clanging, and I jumped up, bewildered for a second.

The church bell was calling the villagers to evening service. The sun was low in the sky now, and still Aunt Frank had not come home.

I washed, and changed out of my

rumpled dress. Tidy again, I sat downstairs awaiting her return, the grandfather clock in the corner remorselessly ticking away the minutes.

14

ON Monday, soon after lunching off cold pork from the day before, I set out for Sherbridge. Aunt Frank had reserved a set of books at the public library, and a post card had arrived that morning to say they awaited her collection.

"Will you be able to manage them, dear?" my aunt had asked. "There are seven altogether, and some of them will be pretty heavy."

"I'll take a shopping basket to carry them in," I said.

My aunt went to the library herself at least once a week, and it was obvious enough that she had thought of asking me to fetch these books as a way of keeping me occupied. It must have been a problem for poor Aunt Frank to have me mooching around the cottage miserably, without enough interest in anything to take me out. Certainly I wouldn't have dreamed of going into Sherbridge on my own account as things were. But in a curious way I felt grateful to Aunt Frank for sending me there, for making me resume a degree of normality.

I walked down to the bus stop outside the village general store, conscious of the odd and often pitying glances from everyone I passed. I should have grown accustomed to this behaviour and I tried to accept it without flinching. In Sherbridge I hoped that I would be able to pass unnoticed, but even there I became aware of occasional long stares, whispered words to a companion. I was recognized! I wanted to turn on my heels and run away, but I made myself stick it out. It would be weeks before I could escape into anonymity.

Suddenly I realized that I was standing in a small back street, looking up at a grey stone building. Unconsciously my footsteps had brought me to the place where Mark was held prisoner. What would he be doing now? This very minute, while I stood outside? Only a few yards separated us. We were so near, and yet so irrevocably cut off from one another. There was no contact between us at all. Somehow I should have to learn to live my life without Mark.

Slowly I turned and walked away.

At the library I collected the books for Aunt Frank, and wandered back to the station to catch the bus home. As I took my place in the queue I was looking across at the theatre where, five years ago, I had gone in a gay party to see Rhoda acting in a play.

I had been waiting for a bus in this very same spot the day Mark had stopped his car and picked me up. That had been the start of our second love affair. I remembered my fierce rush of joy at seeing him and hearing his cheerful voice.

"Going home? Jump in then."

Faint with shock, I realized the words had actually been spoken. Almost the same words that Mark had used.

Derek's red sports car was drawn up at the kerb, and he was holding the door open for me. Unwillingly I got in. I felt very poor company just then, but it would have been too pointedly rude to refuse in front of so many people.

I was surprised that Derek was apparently able to knock off work sharp at five-thirty—it looked as if he was taking his new responsibilities at the factory very lightly.

The traffic was heavy as we drove out of the town, and Derek made no attempt at conversation. But when we turned off at the lane to the village, he asked if I was in a hurry.

"I'd like to have a talk with you, Jan."

I could hardly refuse. "Come in and have a cup of tea," I invited. "Aunt Frank will be pleased to see you."

"No, I meant alone."

"Just as you like."

We drove through the village, and I thought for a moment he was intending to take me to the Buxton house. But he went straight past the gates, up to the top of the hill. Then, abruptly, he turned off by the old quarries.

Involuntarily, I shuddered. It was here that Mark had brought me to tell me the news about Rhoda's murder.

Derek bumped along the uneven track through bushes that must have grown up since the workings had been discontinued. A pair of partridges, startled, flew out of cover and so low over our heads that I felt the draught of their beating wings.

"We'll be quiet here," Derek said, switching off the engine.

Unhurried, he lit a cigarette, inhaling deeply and luxuriously. He leaned back his head and blew the smoke upwards. It hung lazily on the warm still air.

He was looking at me speculatively. "You know, Jan," he began. "I couldn't help noticing yesterday that when your aunt said she didn't believe Mark was . . . responsible for Rhoda's death, *you* didn't say a word."

My heart sank. So we were to have this dragged out again! Is this what he had brought me here to talk about?

"I suppose it was because Aunt Frank rather startled me by saying so."

He smiled faintly. "I thought that must be it. It's horrible, of course . . . we're all so fond of poor old Mark. But we have to be sensible and face facts, haven't we? I mean to say, all that wild talk of your aunt's about it being Aunt Margaret. It's just plain ridiculous!"

"It's not ridiculous at all," I cried hotly, without taking thought.

Derek was looking at me incredulously now. "You really think Aunt Margaret might have done it? What on earth's the matter with you, Jan? Are you so crazy about Mark that you refuse to accept what's perfectly obvious?"

It was a cruel and wicked thing to say. I almost wondered if Derek was quite deliberately trying to hurt me.

I did my best to keep control over my voice, but I know it trembled.

"It seems to me, Derek, that you actually want Mark to be found guilty. I agree it's a horrible idea that his mother killed Rhoda, but why are you so ready to believe it of *him*, and not of *her?*"

"I could just as easily ask you the same thing the other way round," he said quickly. "And don't forget, the police think the way I do. They think it was Mark, too."

"Only because he is letting them. Mark just isn't putting up a fight."

Derek frowned, puzzled. He tossed his half-finished cigarette over the side of the car. "What do you mean—not putting up a fight?"

I didn't answer. I knew that already I

had said too much. Because I couldn't bear to hear Mark so abused, I had really admitted that I believed his mother was the guilty one. I had broken my resolution to keep silent.

Derek asked me again, "What do you mean—Mark isn't putting up a fight?"

Still I said nothing. I looked down, not wanting to meet his eyes. But Derek shot out his hand and took hold of my chin, turning me round to face him.

"You're really convinced that Aunt Margaret killed Rhoda? You think Mark is deliberately protecting her, don't you?"

I stared back at him, unable to deny it. Suddenly he gripped me tightly by the shoulders.

"Jan, you simply must get over this thing you've got about Mark. Whether he's actually found guilty or not, he's no good to you now. Mud sticks, remember."

"What a beastly thing to say!" I twisted away from him. "I love Mark and I don't care what other people think. And he won't be found guilty, because he *isn't* guilty."

It was no more than a defiant gesture. I wished desperately I had the confidence I pretended that Mark would be found innocent.

"Take me home, please Derek." I said sharply. "Aunt Frank will be expecting me."

"All right, all right. In a minute."

He took out his cigarette case again. His hands were shaking, so that he fumbled and dropped one or two on the floor of the car. He left them there, careless.

"Look here, Jan," he went on. "Don't be angry with me. Remember that evening out we had at the 'Chequers'? Why not let's do it again tonight? It would cheer you up."

I was astonished that Derek could even imagine I would go out with him now. Quite apart from the vile things he had said about Mark, couldn't he see I was in no mood for gadding around?

"It's out of the question, Derek," I said shortly.

"You won't give me a chance, will you?" he muttered.

"What do you mean?"

"Surely you must know how I feel, Jan. I'm absolutely crazy about you."

The second cigarette followed the first

out on to the grass, and he snatched my two hands, bending towards me fiercely.

"But Derek," I protested. "It's impossible. Can't you understand . . . ?"

"I understand one thing as far as you're concerned, darling. I'm madly in love with you. As soon as I saw you again that first evening, I said to myself, 'This is the girl for me.'"

I struggled away from him, pressing myself against the side of the car. But he grabbed me again and forced an arm round my shoulders.

"My God, I love you, Jan," he murmured, clawing me to him. When I objected, he gave a smothered laugh, holding me so firmly that I could hardly move. "You haven't been very forthcoming, have you, darling? But if it's marriage you're waiting for, that's okay by me. In fact it's what I want myself."

I was amazed by this sudden stark proposal and Derek must have thought my shocked silence was a sort of half assent. But when his lips touched mine I revolted, finding the sudden strength to push him away from me.

"No!" I cried furiously. "How can you

behave like this with Mark locked up in gaol? How can you?"

Now his anger more than matched my own. He let me go, savagely punching his fist on the leather seat at his side. "Mark," he yelled. "That's all you can say. *Mark! Mark! Mark!* I tell you, I'm sick to death of hearing that name."

Again I was rigid in my seat, staring at Derek wide-eyed.

"Mark took Rhoda away from me," he went on, almost sobbing in his rage. "I'd have made a go of it with her—we understood one another. Everything was going nicely, and then she was dazzled by the Galbraith knighthood! But Mark couldn't hold her for long, could he? He wasn't man enough, I tell you . . ."

He glared across at me, his eyes blazing. "You!" he spat. "I suppose you latched on to Mark because you thought the factory would eventually belong to him. Well, it won't now, will it? Mark is on trial for murder, and I'm in sole charge. You backed the wrong horse, Jan."

He filled me with loathing. I couldn't utter a word.

"Your beloved Mark is very clever when

it comes to wheedling his way into favour. Uncle Lionel was properly taken in by him. Just because he had a few cheap-jack ideas to help get the business out of the red! And then you come along, and Mark makes eyes at you. Well, now he's landed with a murder charge. Let him talk his way out of that one."

Maddened, I found my voice. "I'll not sit here and listen to this . . . this filth," I cried. I wrenched at the door catch, but Derek reached over and caught my arm.

"No you don't, darling. I want to talk to you."

"Let me go," I said fiercely, wondering what I could do. In this isolated spot it was useless to jump out and run. Derek would easily catch up with me in a few yards.

He settled back comfortably, an odd smile on his lips.

"That's no way to behave to a man who's just proposed to you. I'm still ready to marry you, Jan. I like a girl to have a bit of spirit. Rhoda was quite a spitfire too in her way. I used to enjoy it with her . . ."

Somehow I managed to control my voice. I tried to talk reasonably.

"Derek, will you drive me back to Mead Cottage, and we'll forget this conversation. It's obvious that you've got it in for Mark, but it's no use trying to work that off on me. I happen to love him. And I believe absolutely, without any doubt in my mind at all, that Mark is innocent . . ."

"So you think his mother did it," Derek said scornfully. "Do you really imagine a woman in her fifties could strangle a tough egg like Rhoda with her bare hands? You can think again, sweetheart. Rhoda was a hellcat when she was roused. Why, she fought me like a mad thing . . ."

He pulled himself up abruptly, looking startled. Icy claws gripped me as the significance of his words sank in. I shivered violently.

Derek said quickly, "I mean, Rhoda was a fighter. She'd have been too much for the old girl."

I turned on him. *"You* did it, didn't you? You killed Rhoda!"

"Don't be absurd, Jan." But the sudden swift narrowing of his eyes told a different story.

"Why is it nobody thought of you before? You had as good a motive as anyone, didn't you? You hated Rhoda because she threw you over."

"The dirty rotten bitch!"

The words seemed to spring out of him, as though a leash had been on his tongue too long. Then suddenly he became very still. He sat staring ahead with glazed, unseeing eyes. It was as if he didn't know I was there.

"What happened?" I asked in a whisper.

Derek stirred slightly, and a small twisted smile touched the corners of his mouth.

For the moment I was too stunned to feel any sense of fear. "What happened?" I asked again.

Derek appeared to be in a sort of trance. He began to speak in a flat, stilted voice.

"I was just driving off from the pub when I saw her walking towards me in the rain. I'd thought she was dead and I couldn't believe my eyes, but I would have known her anywhere—the way she moved. 'Hallo, Derek,' she said, and she smiled—just as if it had been the day before when I had last seen her, just as if we hadn't all thought she was dead. I hated her, but I couldn't help being excited, seeing her again. She got into the car and I drove off, away from the village, to somewhere we could talk.

"I heard all about her leaving Mark and how clever she'd been in disappearing during that hotel fire. Then she told me how she'd squeezed a cheque for five hundred quid out of Aunt Margaret. She said that she was off back to London to find another man. That made me see red. I couldn't bear the idea of someone else touching her." Derek's voice had been getting louder and louder; now it began to break. "I told her *I'd* give her money. I promised to find her a flat where I could come to see her. I begged her, but she wouldn't have it . . ." His eyes were glaring now, not seeing me, but re-living what had happened. He was trembling violently. "She laughed at me. She said I wasn't worth staying in this back of beyond for. She laughed in my face. I hated her! *I hated her!*"

His voice stopped suddenly and he was quite still again, his nightmare vision played to its end. It seemed as if it had been a relief to him to talk—that he was glad to have unburdened himself at last.

It was obvious to me that there was madness in Derek. I was *almost* touched with pity for him. He had been obsessed about Rhoda for years, and she had toyed with his fierce passion, using it when it suited her, then tossing it back at him. I could imagine how her laughter had goaded Derek that night, incensing him with such mad fury that in desperation he had gripped her by the throat, and choked the life out of her. If anyone deserved to die, Rhoda did. She had been utterly worthless. I could indeed almost feel pity for the demented man who had killed her. But I couldn't forget that Derek was letting Mark suffer for it.

A surge of excitement flooded through me as I realized that at last Mark would be cleared of the charge against him. Mark would be freed!

"Derek," I said gently, as if talking to a child. "Derek, you must tell all this to the police—just as you have told me. It isn't right for you to let Mark take the blame . . ."

The sound of Mark's name was like a trigger to Derek. He suddenly jerked out of his dream state, immediately alert.

"No!" he cried. "Mark's going to carry the can for that lot."

I had thought that Derek's trance-like confession had been a sign of defeat, of humble resignation. But instantly I realized my mistake. There was nothing subdued about him now. He was like a tiger ready to pounce. I was shot through with fear.

"Mark deserves to suffer for all he has taken away from me," Derek was shouting. "Rhoda, and the factory, and then you. He's always been so damned clever—everybody has always liked him best. But now he's going to pay for it. They all think he killed Rhoda—I made sure of that. I took her body out to sea in Mark's boat and left her hat in it. And I tore up the cheque she got from Aunt Margaret and put the bits in the ashtray in the back of his car, next day. That's enough evidence to convict him. Nobody's going to believe it was me, or Aunt Margaret, or anyone else. Mark's going to be the one to pay."

Derek's bitter hatred of Mark, I realized, was as much a part of his madness as his thwarted desire for Rhoda had been. There was no hope that I could persuade him to give himself up for Mark's sake. I realized, too, that now I was in grave danger. I knew that Derek was the killer. Feverishly I tried to think how I could save myself.

Derek must have read my mind. He began to laugh—a hollow, mirthless chuckle that pricked every nerve in my body.

"You're not going to tell them, Jan. I only told *you* what happened because you'd guessed. But no one else will know. They'll think it was Mark."

"Of course they won't. You can't stop them from finding out now."

His blazing eyes mocked me. "Oh Jan, how naive you are! I'm not going to *let* you tell them. What I've done once, I can do again."

"You wouldn't dare. You'd never get away with it." Rigid with fear I sought around wildly for something I could say to convince him. "People must have seen us together . . . in the bus queue . . . driving through the village."

"But I wouldn't try to deny it. I shall break the sad news that you were stricken with grief about Mark, and that I couldn't stop you throwing yourself over the edge."

"Nobody would believe that. You're mad . . ."

As he gripped me by the shoulders I screamed in terror.

There was a shout from somewhere behind us. We both swung round. A glint of silver caught the evening sun. Two uniformed figures broke from cover and started running towards us.

"The police!" Derek gasped. "They're on to me."

Instantly he reached forward and started the car.

"They'll not get me, Jan, and I'll take you with me. At least Mark won't have you."

The police were so near, but already Derek had the car moving, accelerating towards the edge of the quarry. With desperate inspiration I grabbed the ignition key. In one quick twist I had it out and flung it into the bushes. The engine coughed into silence, and the car rolled to a standstill only a few yards from the brink.

Cursing violently, Derek vaulted over the car door just as one of the police closed on him. They struggled together for a moment, grunting and gasping. Then with a savage thrust Derek pushed the policeman back. As the man stumbled, trying to regain his balance, Derek looked around wildly. He saw the second officer was almost upon him. Cornered, Derek rushed to the edge of the quarry, and in a single movement hurled himself into space.

I closed my eyes, overwhelmed with sick giddiness.

It seemed a long time before silence returned to the quarry. My ears were filled with a rattling, scraping clatter that I only realized later was the sound of dislodged stones and gravel tumbling to the bottom of the almost sheer rock face.

When I opened my eyes, the policeman was standing at the spot where Derek had jumped, looking down. Then, slowly and carefully, he started to lower himself over the edge and out of sight.

"Are you all right, Miss?"

The second policeman was bending over the car, eyeing me anxiously.

Clutching at his arm, I cried out hysterically, *"He* did it. Do you know that? He killed Rhoda . . ."

He patted my shoulder. "There, there," he said placatingly. "We've heard and seen enough, Miss. Don't you worry yourself about it."

He allowed me a minute to pull myself together, then he said gently, "Will you come over to our car, Miss? I'll have to radio a report about this."

I found it difficult to make my legs carry me. He helped me, almost holding me up. As we went slowly across the short turf and through the bushes, I was babbling, "Thank goodness you arrived. How did you know . . . ?"

"We've been on his tail all day, Miss. The sergeant had a tip off last evening. We were told to keep a close eye on him, to see if we could dig anything up."

The police car was hidden in the bushes, drawn up off the track. The constable put me in the rear seat, and radioed headquarters. Dully, I heard him giving details.

He turned back to me. "The sergeant will be out here soon, Miss. I'm afraid you'll have to wait until he arrives."

I nodded. "Of course," I said faintly. "I understand."

We heard a slight rustling sound, and realized the other policeman was coming back. His colleague got out of the car and went to meet him. I watched the two men talking together just out of earshot.

I couldn't hear a word they said, but their gestures were plain enough to tell me everything. Derek was dead. Derek was at the bottom of the quarry, smashed beyond recognition.

15

ONLY an hour or two at the most separated me from Mark, and yet the waiting seemed interminable. I had been living through days of dull despair, but now I was seething with impatient longing for him to come.

Sergeant Hayes had himself driven me back to Mead Cottage when everything was finished at the quarry. When all the questions had been asked, and when Derek's smashed body had been recovered and taken away by an ambulance. The sergeant came in to have a word with Aunt Frank, and it was only then that I learned of her part in the affair, and realized just how much I owed her.

The lunch party for Derek the day before had been a put up job, a clever scheme designed to sound him out.

"I was ready to accept the fact that Mark was innocent," my aunt explained. "I've always had a very high regard for that young man, and your own absolute

274

faith in him convinced me he couldn't be guilty. Therefore it had to be someone else. You had already eliminated the man in London, and I just couldn't believe it was Margaret Galbraith. Oh, I know that her motives were as strong as Mark's, and that all the evidence applying to him could just as well fit her. But somehow I knew that she *couldn't* have done it. I'm afraid my reason for being so sure doesn't flatter her—it was a conviction that Margaret Galbraith would never have *sullied* herself to the extent of strangling the girl, and disposing of the body. So who else could it possibly be? Then the other day Sally mentioned that Rhoda had once been Derek's girl friend, and I began to suspect he might be the one. So I invited him to lunch. When Derek was here he behaved in such a peculiar manner that I was sure I was on to something."

"I did think he was acting rather strangely," I said. "He seemed terribly upset when you were suggesting that it might not be Mark, but Lady Galbraith."

"Yes indeed. The very idea seemed to enrage him, though I didn't imagine he had any special affection for his aunt. He usually ignored her when she was visiting the Buxtons. On the other hand, Derek was bitterly resentful of his cousin—even I couldn't help noticing that. Although Derek was pretending to be very sorry for Mark yesterday, I suspected that he was secretly rather exultant, and couldn't bear the idea that anyone but Mark might be thought guilty. When I went on to talk about modern police methods, Derek seemed to be rattled, and he left us as soon as he decently could. And what do you think he did then?" she asked triumphantly. "He went straight back home and started giving the inside of his car a thorough scouring. He went over it with a vacuum cleaner, and then soap and water, as if his life depended on it."

"So that's where you went yesterday afternoon?"

"Yes, I did a bit of sleuthing. I slipped in at the back gate of the Buxtons' house, and crept round by the garage. Derek was hard at it already, so I realized my remarks must really have frightened him. That was good enough for me."

"So you came back here for your car

and went in to Sherbridge to tell Sergeant Hayes?"

She nodded. "I didn't like to say anything to you at the time, Jan, in case it didn't work out as I hoped."

"Between ourselves," the sergeant cut in, "what your aunt told us was good enough for me, too, but only personally, you understand. As a policeman I needed more to go on than that. A fellow has a perfect right to clean out his car if he wants to—you can't arrest him for that. So I decided we'd better keep a close watch on friend Buxton, in the hope that he gave himself away. He obliged quicker than I expected, though I'm afraid it must have been pretty grim for you, Miss Prior, sitting there in the car with him."

I said weakly, "If I'd known two of your men were within earshot, I wouldn't have been so terrified . . ."

"Well, it's all over now," he said. "And if you had known we were behind you, maybe it wouldn't have worked out like it did. Considering everything, I think Derek Buxton's death may prove to be the best way out for everyone concerned."

Sergeant Hayes left us then. "I must see

about getting that young man back to you as soon as possible," he said with a smile. "You'll never forgive me if I delay."

I wanted to go in to Sherbridge with him, but he resisted the idea, refusing quite firmly.

"I'll send him home in one of our cars," he said. "Better for you to wait for him here."

Mark's release from custody wasn't going to solve everything magically, with the wave of a wand. But it was difficult for me to contain my surging happiness. It was hard to bring my mind to the trail of problems that would still be left behind.

Lady Galbraith! I flushed with shame as I remembered how convinced I had been that she had murdered Rhoda. It was a dreadful, unforgivable thing to believe of someone. Yet Mark too, her own son, had believed it. Her character and behaviour had given him cause. And she on her part had disowned him since his arrest, as if wiping him out of her life. Was it because she thought Mark guilty? Or was it just that she refused to have the smallest connection with him in what, to her, was an unutterably sordid position? After such a lack of sympathy and understanding between mother and son, was it possible they could ever again achieve a reasonable relationship?

And then there was the effect of Derek's death upon his family—Sally, and Mr. and Mrs. Buxton. In his present condition could Lionel Buxton survive the shock of what had happened?

I asked my aunt who would tell them the news. Would she perhaps telephone Sally?

"No, Jan. That job is best left to the police. Sergeant Hayes knows the situation there. He'll make sure that the news is broken as carefully as possible."

"But what will it do to Mr. Buxton? Surely it might well be . . . too much for him?"

My aunt looked thoughtful. "No," she said slowly, "I don't think it will. You see, Jan, it has been obvious to me, being so intimate with them over the years, that Derek had always been something of a disappointment to Dolly and Lionel. Not that they'd ever admit it to a soul, of course—hardly even to themselves. But Derek was never anything like as close to them as his sister. Sally has brought so much happiness to her uncle and aunt that I think it helped to cover up Derek's lack of affection. They treated him like a son, and he repaid them by expecting everything and giving nothing."

"He expected that the factory would be his," I said.

"I know. I suppose it was understandable that Lionel wanted Derek to be able to take over from him eventually. He had always tried to prepare the boy for responsibility. But I think Lionel knew in his heart that Derek would never make the grade. He was always so casual in his attitude to work—he'd never make the least effort. When Lionel had his stroke, Derek just floundered around ineffectively. If Dolly hadn't thought of asking Mark to help them out, I think the business would have folded up." My aunt shook her head. "Poor Mark! I'm afraid he's got his work cut out now. I only hope things haven't got in too much of a mess since Derek's been in charge."

That was another of the problems still to be solved.

During the next hour I changed my

dress twice, and fussed around in front of the looking-glass. I wanted to look my tip-top best for Mark. Aunt Frank pretended not to notice anything. I realized she noticed what she wanted to notice, heard what she wanted to hear.

She heard the police car even before I did—my ears must have been straining too hard. Aunt Frank jumped to her feet suddenly, and strode over to the door of her study.

"This won't do," she announced. "I've got work to be getting on with. See you later."

The door closed firmly behind her, and only then did I hear the sound of tyres slithering to a stop on the loose surface of the lane outside.

I wanted to dash to the front door and fling it open. I wanted to throw myself into Mark's arms. But curiously, now that the wonderful moment I had been longing for was here, I just couldn't move. My legs were paralysed.

Already I could hear the police car backing away down the lane. The gate clicked, and slammed shut again.

Mark's quick, impatient footsteps on the

path brought me back to life. I rushed forward.

As I dragged open the door, light from behind me streamed forth, picking out his tall figure in the porch, one hand raised to ring the bell.

"Oh Mark!"

He reached out for me, and suddenly I was in his arms.

"Jan, oh my darling!" His lips were against my hair. "Thank God you are safe! What a terrible time you have had."

We had hardly moved when Aunt Frank called out to us a few minutes later.

"You'd better bring him in off the front step, Jan."

She was in the sitting room, her eyes twinkling. In a gruff masculine way she held out a hand. "It's good to see you here again, Mark."

"It's good to *be* here, Miss Prior. And it's all thanks to you." He put an arm round my shoulder. "We both owe you more than I can ever say."

Firmly, almost ruthlessly, Aunt Frank made it clear that she wanted and would accept no gratitude. "I'm going to make some coffee," she said. "And you'll be needing something to eat, young man."

"No thank you. I'm not hungry. The police have been looking after me very well."

Sergeant Hayes had told Mark all about my escapade in Derek's car before he had jumped to his death, and how Aunt Frank's suspicions of Derek had caused the police to be tailing him.

"If it hadn't been for her . . ." Mark said, and I shuddered with him.

When my aunt appeared again with a tray of coffee things, she was very brisk and matter-of-fact.

"I've been thinking," she said. "Would you care to stay here tonight, Mark? It's late for you to be going home, and your mother may be in bed. Better leave seeing her until the morning. We can put you up, after a fashion."

Mark thanked Aunt Frank soberly. "It . . . it won't be an easy re-union. There's a lot that has to be said between my mother and me." His face had clouded over, and I knew just how much he was dreading this meeting.

I came back to it later, when we were

alone again. "Mark . . . your mother. Is there anything I can do? Shall I come with you tomorrow?"

He smiled down at me, and drew me closer to him.

"Thank you, darling. You're going to *have* to help me with Mother, perhaps more than you know. But I think I had better see her alone first." He paused for a moment, deep in thought. "It's going to be difficult for us Jan . . ."

"We'll find a way, Mark. You mustn't worry."

But he shook his head. "We've got to face up to it, darling. Mother is Mother. She isn't ever going to change very much. Unless we are going to turn our backs on her completely, we shall have to adapt ourselves to her, not she to us."

"I know," I soothed him. "I understand."

His dark blue eyes regarded me gravely. I saw his face was pale.

"Do you realize, Jan, what a state things had got to between us? My mother and I, each believed the other was capable of murder. How did we ever come to have so little faith in one another, so little trust?"

"You'll have to make a new start, Mark. Begin again."

He nodded. "Dad was always too easy-going with her, I'm afraid, and I have followed in his footsteps. We always let Mother have her own way about every-thing, because it seemed to mean so much to her. But I am to blame for the situation between us just as much as she is—more so really, because poor Mother's horizons are limited by this dominating pride of hers."

I knew now what I had suspected before. Mark's apparent filial devotion, his rather extreme attentiveness to his mother, had been something of a façade. It concealed the absence of a genuine, natural love. With guilt in his heart he had been trying to make up for his inability to feel the real affection her cold and selfish nature wouldn't allow.

His voice cold with determination, Mark said, "Mother has got to be *made* to understand that she must accept people as they are, not demand that they should be as she wants them."

"Don't be too hard on her, Mark darling."

I was discovering how true it is that you can afford to be magnanimous when the world is at your feet. I had Mark now. That was everything I wanted in life. Lady Galbraith was to be pitied. She hardly possessed a real friend in the world. Her high-handed disdain over the years had driven people from her.

I resolved that I would offer her my friendship. Somehow I would equip myself with all the patience and understanding needed to win her over. All the effort would be on my side. I would expect nothing from her other than acceptance of me as Mark's wife.

I was taking her son away from her. That was a lot to take from even the most richly endowed woman.

Suddenly I felt there wasn't a problem I couldn't solve. Everything was going to be possible, now.

"Darling Jan," Mark was saying, "I wanted to offer you a bed of roses, but at the moment you'll only feel the thorns. It's not just Mother, but the factory too. That must be in a hell of a mess. I've got to keep things going there—for Uncle Lionel's sake. Especially now . . ."

286

"Of course you must. And Mark . . . *I* could help." I told him my idea of standing in as his secretary. "Just for the time being," I urged. "Until you get straightened out."

He looked at me in amazement; then he burst into laughter. It was the first joyful sound from Mark for such a long time.

"Janice, my lovely Janice!" he cried. "I bring you nothing but problems, and you still come up smiling. How can you accept so little?"

"I love you, Mark. It's *you* I want. As long as I have you nothing else matters."

And then his arms were around me, and he was kissing me. And my world was complete.

DONCASTER
LIBRARY SERVICE 1 9 JAN 1995

We hope this Large Print edition gives you the pleasure and enjoyment we ourselves experienced in its publication.

There are now more than 2,000 titles available in this ULVERSCROFT Large print Series. Ask to see a Selection at your nearest library.

The Publisher will be delighted to send you, free of charge, upon request a complete and up-to-date list of all titles available.

Ulverscroft Large Print Books Ltd.
The Green, Bradgate Road
Anstey
Leicestershire
LE7 7FU
England

GUIDE
TO THE COLOUR CODING
OF
ULVERSCROFT BOOKS

Many of our readers have written to us expressing their appreciation for the way in which our colour coding has assisted them in selecting the Ulverscroft books of their choice.

To remind everyone of our colour coding— this is as follows:

BLACK COVERS
Mysteries

*

BLUE COVERS
Romances

*

RED COVERS
Adventure Suspense and General Fiction

*

ORANGE COVERS
Westerns

*

GREEN COVERS
Non-Fiction

ROMANCE TITLES
in the
Ulverscroft Large Print Series

THE SHADOWS
OF THE CROWN TITLES
in the
Ulverscroft Large Print Series

The Trial of Charles I   *C. V. Wedgwood*
Royal Flush   *Margaret Irwin*
The Sceptre and the Rose   *Doris Leslie*
Mary II: Queen of England *Hester Chapman*
That Enchantress   *Doris Leslie*
The Princess of Celle   *Jean Plaidy*
Caroline the Queen   *Jean Plaidy*
The Third George   *Jean Plaidy*
The Great Corinthian   *Doris Leslie*
Victoria in the Wings   *Jean Plaidy*
The Captive of Kensington Palace
        Jean Plaidy
The Queen and Lord 'M'   *Jean Plaidy*
The Queen's Husband   *Jean Plaidy*
The Widow of Windsor   *Jean Plaidy*
Bertie and Alix   *Graham and Heather Fisher*
The Duke of Windsor   *Ursula Bloom*

FICTION TITLES
in the
Ulverscroft Large Print Series

Enquiry	*Dick Francis*
Flying Finish	*Dick Francis*
Forfeit	*Dick Francis*
High Stakes	*Dick Francis*
In The Frame	*Dick Francis*
Knock Down	*Dick Francis*
Risk	*Dick Francis*
Band of Brothers	*Ernest K. Gann*
Twilight For The Gods	*Ernest K. Gann*
Army of Shadows	*John Harris*
The Claws of Mercy	*John Harris*
Getaway	*John Harris*
Winter Quarry	*Paul Henissart*
East of Desolation	*Jack Higgins*
In the Hour Before Midnight	*Jack Higgins*
Night Judgement at Sinos	*Jack Higgins*
Wrath of the Lion	*Jack Higgins*
Air Bridge	*Hammond Innes*
A Cleft of Stars	*Geoffrey Jenkins*
A Grue of Ice	*Geoffrey Jenkins*
Beloved Exiles	*Agnes Newton Keith*
Passport to Peril	*James Leasor*
Goodbye California	*Alistair MacLean*
South By Java Head	*Alistair MacLean*
All Other Perils	*Robert MacLeod*
Dragonship	*Robert MacLeod*
A Killing in Malta.	*Robert MacLeod*
A Property in Cyprus	*Robert MacLeod*

NON-FICTION TITLES
in the
Ulverscroft Large Print Series